KU-447-232

MURDER IN THE CATHEDRAL
AND
THE COCKTAIL PARTY

Text and Performance

WILLIAM TYDEMAN

MACMILLAN
EDUCATION

QUEEN MARGARET COLLEGE LIBRARY

© William Tydeman 1988

All rights reserved. No reproduction, copy or transmission
of this publication may be made without written permission.

No paragraph of this publication may be reproduced, copied
or transmitted save with written permission or in accordance
with the provisions of the Copyright Act 1956 (as amended),
or under the terms of any licence permitting limited copying
issued by the Copyright Licensing Agency, 33–4 Alfred Place,
London WC1E 7DP.

Any person who does any unauthorised act in relation to
this publication may be liable to criminal prosecution and
civil claims for damages.

First published 1988

Published by
MACMILLAN EDUCATION LTD
Houndmills, Basingstoke, Hampshire RG21 2XS
and London
Companies and representatives
throughout the world

Typeset by Wessex Typesetters
(Division of The Eastern Press Ltd)
Frome, Somerset

Printed in Hong Kong

British Library Cataloguing in Publication Data
Tydeman, William
  Murder in the cathedral and The Cocktail
  party.——(Text and performance).
  1. Eliot, T.S.——Dramatic works
  I. Title   II. Series
  822'.912   PS3509.L43
ISBN 0-333-42302-X

CONTENTS

Illustrations will be found in Part Two.

ACKNOWLEDGEMENTS

My thanks are due once again to the General Editor and to Beverley Tarquini for their advice, patience and encouragement, and to my colleagues in the Department of English at the University College of North Wales for undertaking duties respite from which enabled me to take a term's Study Leave in the summer of 1987. I am also indebted to the authors of the invaluable books, articles and reviews cited in the text and in the list of suggested reading at the end of the book. References to Eliot's works are taken with permission from the *Collected Poems and Plays* (1969), from *Selected Essays* (1932, enlarged edn, 1951) and from *On Poetry and Poets* (1957).

The author and publishers wish to thank the following who have kindly given permission for the use of copyright material.

Faber and Faber Ltd. and Harcourt Brace Jovanovich, Inc. for excerpts from; *Murder in the Cathedral* by T. S. Eliot, copyright 1935 by Harcourt Brace, Inc. renewed 1963 by T. S. Eliot; *The Cocktail Party* by T. S. Eliot, copyright 1950 by T. S. Eliot, renewed 1978 by Esme Valerie Eliot; *The Family Reunion* by T. S. Eliot, copyright 1939 by T. S. Eliot, renewed 1967 by Esme Valerie Eliot; 'Dialogue on Dramatic Poetry' from *Selected Essays* by T. S. Eliot, copyright 1950 by Harcourt Brace Jovanovich, Inc., renewed 1978 by Esme Valerie Eliot; and Faber and Faber Ltd. for excerpts from *On Poetry and Poets* by T. S. Eliot.

Every effort has been made to trace all the copyright holders but if any have been inadvertently overlooked the publishers will be pleased to make the necessary arrangement at the first opportunity.

GENERAL EDITOR'S PREFACE

For many years a mutual suspicion existed between the theatre director and the literary critic of drama. Although in the first half of the century there were important exceptions, such was the rule. A radical change of attitude, however, has taken place over the last thirty years. Critics and directors now increasingly recognise the significance of each other's work and acknowledge their growing awareness of interdependence. Both interpret the same text, but do so according to their different situations and functions. Without the director, the designer and the actor, a play's existence is only partial. They revitalise the text with action, enabling the drama to live fully at each performance. The academic critic investigates the script to elucidate its textual problems, understand its conventions and discover how it operates. He may also propose his view of the work, expounding what he considers to be its significance.

Dramatic texts belong therefore to theatre and to literature. The aim of the "Text and Performance' series is to achieve a fuller recognition of how both enhance our enjoyment of the play. Each volume follows the same basic pattern. Part One provides a critical introduction to the plays under discussion, using the techniques and criteria of the literary critic in examining the manner in which the work operates through language, imagery and action. Part Two takes the enquiry further into the plays' theatricality by focusing on selected productions so as to illustrate points of contrast and comparison in the interpretation of different directors and actors, and to demonstrate how the plays have worked on the stage. In this way the series seeks to provide a lively and informative introduction to major plays in their text and performance.

MICHAEL SCOTT

PART ONE: TEXT

1 INTRODUCTION

It is one of the better paradoxes of literary history that the British, popularly labelled a phlegmatic and inhibited people, should have produced one of the world's most dynamic and impressive dramatic literatures. It is one further irony of this achievement that a somewhat retiring and reticent American of English affiliations should have carried out some of the more durable experiments seen on the stage of his adopted country between 1930 and 1950. By training and temperament T. S. Eliot was one of the unlikeliest playwrights ever born, and his sustained interest in drama and the making of plays cannot be attributed to a need to mythologise a flamboyant personality as in the case of Oscar Wilde, to Bernard Shaw's skill at verbalising social and moral dialectics, or to an innately theatrical method of conveying ironic perceptions as with J. M. Synge. Eliot appears to have come to the theatre by a predominantly cerebral route, working out the problems of drama coolly and rationally, an approach which has always laid his plays open to the charge that they are coldly conceived and frigidly executed. Few readers or playgoers find Eliot's characters rich in human interest; the power of his presentations only rarely inspires that *frisson* achieved when dialogue and stage picture fuse to encapsulate a psychological truth apprehended not merely intellectually but through the senses. At their best Eliot's plays remind us that major drama consists above all of simplification and pattern, of forms extracted from the flux of life and given permanent significance, but at their worst they can seem pallid and austere theorems, sadly deficient in the illustrative colour and detail which adds sparkle to the drabbest formulations. As Kenneth Tynan, noting the novel emphasis on love in Eliot's last play, *The Elder Statesman* (1958) remarked, 'Often in the past, as the latest Eliot unfolded chill and chaste before us, we have inwardly murmured, "Poor Tom's a-cold".'

Yet these plays, like those of Samuel Beckett, also remind us that effective drama does not depend solely on exciting story lines, psychologically penetrating character portraits or the accurately reproduced situations of everyday life. Although during the course of his dramatic career Eliot shifted his position on several cherished dicta, he never ceased to denigrate the stock ingredients of contemporary commercial theatre as being inadequate to convey the more profound implications of the human condition to which he believed drama should be constantly alerting the spectator's attention. Eliot sought in his writings for the stage to pierce the veil of the ephemeral and insignificant in daily existence in order to disclose those eternal truths which the trivia and impedimenta of our mortal lives cover up. His aim was to expose the deeper, more permanent aspects of life by releasing drama from the stranglehold of the material, the concrete and the everyday in order to reassert its ancient right to bring to our consciousness the immaterial, the intangible and the everlasting. It was a lofty, even an esoteric ambition, and not one in which a high degree of success might have been anticipated in a society increasingly obsessed with the here-and-now and the matter-of-fact. That Eliot achieved even a limited success in this quest says much for his tact, awareness and sensitivity, even if these morally commendable qualities are not usually felt to be among the criteria essential to stage credibility.

But of course it was Eliot's decision to cast almost the whole of his dramatic output in verse form which accounted for a major part of the interest shown in his work by audiences and critics. The mirage of a revitalised and regenerated poetic drama began to stimulate both playwrights and poets almost as soon as the Elizabethan and Jacobean actuality faded from view around the middle of the 17th century, and for some 250 years thereafter valiant attempts were made to emulate the combination of compelling theatricality and sublime rhetoric so admirably demonstrated

in *Dr Faustus, Hamlet* or *The White Devil.* Dryden's *All for Love,*
Addison's *Cato,* Dr Johnson's *Irene,* Coleridge's *Remorse,*
Shelley's *The Cenci,* Byron's *Cain,* Tennyson's *The Cup,*
Browning's *Strafford,* Stephen Phillips's *Paolo and Francesca*
and countless pieces like them were bold attempts to restore
the languishing form of the verse play to the health and
strength it appeared to have enjoyed in its heyday, but few of
their authors took into account the gradually widening gap
between the everyday colloquial English of their time and the
often inflated, pseudo-'Jacobethan' style in which they felt
obliged to write their self-consciously 'poetic' masterpieces.
Where a Jacobean tragedy could modulate without incongruity
from

> I recover like a spent taper for a flash
> And instantly go out

to

> I have caught/An everlasting cold . . .

or Shakespeare dovetail into Lear's final heart-rending
speech the homely request

> Pray you, undo this button . . .

their successors too often either denied their speakers all
traces of common parlance, so that it became impossible to
regard the *dramatis personae* as creatures capable of mortal
existence, or else through the importation of current idioms
created conflict when they juxtaposed them with what might
be termed 'Playgoers' Tudor'.

One of many striking instances is found in J. Westland
Marston's Drury Lane tragedy of 1842, *The Patrician's
Daughter,* in which a courageous (or foolhardy) dramatist
confronted the possibility of creating a blank-verse drama on
the Shakespearean model set in contemporary society and
exploring the very Victorian theme of class prejudice. The
oddity of having personages in top hats and crinolines

discoursing in terms of 'prithee' and 'forsooth' – 'Fie, fie, my
Lord!' says the heroine to her father who responds, 'Be it so,
chit!' – is only exceeded by Marston's efforts to inject
nineteenth-century commonplaces into speeches fabricated in
an alien register which simply will not assimilate them:

> Not out yet, Mabel? Should you thus permit
> The freshness of the morning to escape?
> It counts three hours since noon.

Not only does the iambic pentameter maintain a stultifying
grip on the natural movement of the language here; there is
simply no way in which these remarks can be rendered
casual or credible. One ends a perusal of *The Patrician's
Daughter* endorsing the views of Sam Weller Senior: 'Poetry's
unnat'ral; no man ever talked poetry 'cept a beadle on boxin'
day'.

Apart from those playwrights who explored the limited
potential for drama of the Augustan couplet, scarcely any of
those who essayed the poetic play between 1660 and 1900
saw fit to resist the fatal allure of blank verse and Elizabethan
poetic diction; indeed, some of them seem to have looked
upon this nexus as the goal to which they should legitimately
be aspiring. Coleridge, whose *Remorse* was performed at
Drury Lane in 1813, made no secret in his *Table-Talk* (1835)
that his aim had been pastiche:

> There's such divinity doth hedge our Shakespear round, that we
> cannot even imitate his style. I tried to imitate his manner in the
> *Remorse*, and, when I had done, I found that I had been tracking
> Beaumont and Fletcher and Massinger instead.

The dubious end product of *successfully* following Shakespeare
is nowhere better demonstrated than in Shelley's tragedy,
The Cenci, often considered among the best examples of a
neo-Elizabethan verse play, yet how can one praise a work
wholeheartedly which contains speeches that recall nothing
so much as modern reproductions of antique furniture?

> My God! Can it be possible I have
> To die so suddenly? So young to go
> Under the obscure, cold, rotting, wormy ground!
> To be nailed down into a narrow place;
> To see no more sweet sunshine; hear no more
> Blithe voice of living thing; muse not again
> Upon familiar thoughts, sad, yet thus lost –
> How fearful! to be nothing! or to be . . .
> What? Oh, where am I? Let me not go mad!
> Sweet Heaven, forgive weak thoughts! If there should be
> No God, no Heaven, no Earth in the void world;
> The wide, gray, lampless, deep, unpeopled world!
> [p. 118–9]

Reminiscences of *Measure for Measure, Romeo and Juliet* and *King Lear* huddle together for warmth here, but Shelley's adjectival exuberance betrays his basic failure to reanimate the Shakespearean spirit, and in this ineptitude he was far from alone.

Yet one can understand the motives which prompted such valiant assaults on the lofty pinnacle of poetic drama; dramatic language for many seemed to have lost its brilliance and excitement, and as the nineteenth century advanced, more and more plays were couched in the threadbare and colourless diction of a humdrum and materialistic society, a medium suited to describing the lives of ordinary men and women which now formed the favoured dramatic subject matter of the naturalistic school of playwrights. W. B. Yeats voiced the dissatisfaction of a poet starved of bright lyrical language in the theatre, when he described his response to Ibsen's pioneering piece, *A Doll's House* (1879):

> Ibsen has sincerity and logic beyond any writer of our time, and we are all seeking to learn them at his hands; but is he not a good deal less than the greatest of all times, because he lacks beautiful and vivid language? 'Well, well, give me time and you shall hear all about it. If only I had Peter here now' is very like life, is entirely in its place where it comes, and . . . one is moved . . . and yet not moved as if the words themselves could sing and shine.
>
> (*Plays and Controversies*, 1923)

To this line of argument Ibsen had already supplied his own defence in an often-quoted letter written to his English admirer Edmund Gosse in 1874, concerning *Emperor and Galilean*:

> You feel that drama should be in verse, and that the play would have been improved if I had so written it. I must disagree. It is, as you must have seen, a realistic play, and I wanted to make the reader feel that he was sharing in something that really happened. . . . We are no longer living in the age of Shakespeare. . . . Since it was human beings that I wanted to draw, I could not let them speak the language of the gods. . . .   (15 January 1874)

The debate is self-evidently irresolvable, but the deadlock which both Yeats and Eliot set out to break was partly the result of a need to devise a mode of dramatic speech that audiences would find appropriate and credible in the mouths of characters possessing contemporary immediacy, but which could also 'sing and shine' and so release dialogue with a minimum of incongruity from those restraints imposed on it by middle-class social custom and by the realistic conventions of the late nineteenth-century stage. While Yeats confined his experiments in the main to the handling of Irish mythological subject matter intended primarily for a restricted clientèle, Eliot carried his search for a suitable mode of theatrical expression into the lions' den of the commercial playhouse, taking his chance alongside those popular 'French window' comedies of upper middle-class life which his later work so closely resembles.

This boldness came as something of a bombshell to those who had followed the phases by which Eliot had in the first instance come to be a practising dramatist. Unlike Yeats, he had never been involved in theatre management, and had only briefly associated with a dramatic organisation such as the Group Theatre which staged *Sweeney Agonistes* in 1934. Despite what many of his contemporaries regarded as a pronounced theatrical streak in his make-up, there is no evidence that Eliot was ever an ardent playgoer (although he was a devotee of the declining music-hall) and he appears to

have been drawn to drama initially by its affiliations to myth
and ritual, a route no doubt signposted by such pioneering
works of anthropology as Sir James Frazer's *The Golden Bough*,
the writings linking drama and ceremonial by Jane Harrison
and F. M. Cornford, and by discussions of the nature of
Greek tragedy brought to a wider public by the activities of
Professor Gilbert Murray. Eliot's search for his own poetic
voice also led him to a close consideration of the work of
Shakespeare and his contemporaries, not as models but
rather as mentors, and it is noteworthy that for several of his
early poems he adopted the favoured Victorian form of the
dramatic monologue, most notably in the epoch-making *Love
Song of J. Alfred Prufrock*. Moreover, as the late Gareth Lloyd
Evans is at pains to demonstrate in *The Language of Modern
Drama* (1977), the poet's most celebrated work, *The Waste
Land*, is itself formed out of a texture of miniature dramas,
with one piece of dialogue overlapped with another to provide
the effect of a collage. The jettisoning of the original working
title, 'He Do the Police in Different Voices' – a quotation
from Dickens's *Bleak House* – rather obscures this aspect of
the poem.

Eliot's interest in the theatre manifested itself publicly in a
variety of reviews and articles composed in the 1920s where
he wrestled with the theoretical issues and problems arising
from the demands of drama as a genre and those of verse
plays in particular, claiming in the *Athenaeum* for 14 May
1919 that 'the composition of a poetic drama is . . . the most
difficult, the most exhausting task that a poet can set himself'.
In 'The Possibility of a Poetic Drama' published in the *Dial*
for November 1920 he went on to identify 'a legitimate
craving, not restricted to a few persons, which only the verse
play can satisfy', but argued that instead of writing plays
'aimed at the small public which wants "poetry"', writers
should take an already current form of entertainment 'and
subject it to the process which would leave it a form of art'.

Evidence that Eliot was himself experimenting now with
the idea of a verse play is contained in the *Journals* of Arnold
Bennett, the novelist, who on 10 September 1924 recorded
that 'He [Eliot] wanted to write a drama of modern life

(furnished flat sort of people) in a rhythmic prose "perhaps
with certain things in it accentuated by drumbeats". And he
wanted my advice. We arranged that he should do the
scenario and some sample pages of dialogue.' The result was
two specimens – 'Fragments of a Prologue' and 'Fragment of
an Agon' – which featured 'Apeneck Sweeney' of the *Poems*
(1920) and which, after appearing under the title 'Wanna Go
Home, Baby?', were subsequently published as *Sweeney
Agonistes* in 1932. Here the poet went some way towards
forging a new voice for English verse drama by employing
the colloquial cadences of demotic speech in a heightened
and often choric mode, the images and rhythms of popular
song lyrics and jazz, the stylistic conventions of music-hall
patter and the minstrel show, to expose the futility and
hollowness of postwar life among 'furnished flat sort of
people'. These highly stylised, almost expressionistic pieces
were far removed from the general run of naturalistic plays of
the time, emphasising the links between the strangely
menacing boredom of temporal existence and the perennial
relevance of archetypal myths of sterility and death.

Many commentators believe that this work, incomplete as
it is, offered a more promising and stimulating way ahead for
the development of a meaningful 'new drama' than did any
of Eliot's subsequent plays; as it was, nothing quite like
Sweeney Agonistes was to appear outside the brief experiments
of Aude and Isherwood until the '50s and '60s when Samuel
Beckett and Harold Pinter began to exploit the kind of
tactics and techniques Eliot had fleetingly investigated.

But in June 1927 Eliot was baptised and confirmed into
the Anglican Church, and from that point onwards all his
serious work took on a profoundly Christian colouring, so
that it was only a matter of time before his interest in drama
became associated with the service of his new faith. When in
September 1933 he was approached by E. Martin Browne,
another High Churchman, heavily involved in the movement
to revive religious drama in Britain, and invited to produce a
script for a 'pageant' to be presented the following year at
Sadler's Wells Theatre in aid of an ambitious church building
scheme in the London diocese, Eliot was one of the best-

known lay churchmen in the country. *The Rock*, of which only the choruses were reprinted in Eliot's *Collected Poems*, is in part a virtuoso display of a variety of verse forms – pastiches of popular styles, original elegiac-cum-satirical writing in Eliot's own idiosyncratic manner, and choric speeches dependent on the sentiments of Hebrew psalms and the patterns of Christian liturgy. Interspersed are prose scenes by others, some historical vignettes in pageant tradition, others featuring a group of present-day workmen whose task is to build the new churches: some commentators have taken exception to what they regard as a patronisingly superior attitude to the proletariat and their role in the piece. But whatever its faults, *The Rock* achieved the required effect of startling and stimulating those who watched it in an unexpected way; *The Times* found that Eliot had 'created a new thing in the theatre and made smoother the path towards a contemporary poetic drama'.

Thus it was that Eliot came to the composition of *Murder in the Cathedral*, one of the two major works with which this short book is primarily concerned. The circumstances of its production were not entirely dissimilar to those in which *The Rock* took shape, and they will be discussed in more detail in the 'Performance' section of this volume. Once again, Eliot accepted a commission from an organisation with strong religious affiliations – in this case the sponsors of the annual Canterbury Festival – to write a play with a Christian theme for a specific milieu and a specific occasion. True, *The Rock* had required him to cater for a large company of actors, singers, musicians and dancers and his new task was to involve a small restricted cast and a confined, almost inadequate playing space. But at the same time, the auspices under which *Murder in the Cathedral* was first presented in the chapter house at Canterbury Cathedral on 15 June 1935 had more in common with those under which the Sadler's Wells venture had been staged, than with the performance conditions in which all Eliot's subsequent work was to appear.

It was following the unlooked-for success of his Canterbury play that Eliot resolved to carry his campaign for a revitalised

verse drama into the far more treacherous territory of
Shaftesbury Avenue, and allow it, in his own phrase, to
'enter into overt competition with prose drama'. He therefore
decided to steer clear of a historical theme which had
facilitated his use of verse in *Murder in the Cathedral*, and to
dispense with the explicit presence of a chorus as employed
in all his dramatic work up to that point, and set his next
experiment in the present, using a contemporary setting and
characters from everyday life. *The Family Reunion* was
presented, again under E. Martin Browne's direction, at the
Westminster Theatre on 21 March 1939, and while there was
a great deal of interest expressed in Eliot's change of
direction, many critics felt that he had only achieved an
uneasy compromise with the prevailing spirit of naturalism.
But the 'neutral' verse medium in which the piece was
couched sparked off even more debate among poets and
theatre critics, a debate in which the author showed himself
to be as quizzical as anyone.

Eliot's next play did not appear until August 1949 after
the disruptive interval occasioned by World War II; in *The
Cocktail Party* staged at the Edinburgh Festival of that year
the playwright consciously set out to avoid what he regarded
as the errors and weaknesses inherent in *The Family Reunion*.
Since *The Cocktail Party* constitutes the other major text to be
examined in these pages, little more requires to be said at
this stage: it certainly has a claim to be considered as Eliot's
most successful attempt to combine the externals of the
typical commercial product of the English stage between
about 1920 and 1950 with those deeper spiritual concerns
which the writer so consistently made the subject of his art,
and to create a viable theatrical language which could pass
unobtrusively from the discussion of everyday commonplaces
to the transmission of concepts for which the accustomed
vocabulary and rhythms of colloquial diction would be totally
inadequate. It will be part of our business to assess how
considerable an achievement that was.

2 DRAMA AND DOCTRINE

It is impossible to ignore the fact that the substance of all
Eliot's dramatic work produced after *Sweeney Agonistes* is
rooted in the teachings and beliefs of the Christian religion.
Even if we knew nothing of Eliot's personal biography or of
the circumstances in which *The Rock* and *Murder in the
Cathedral* in particular were composed, the themes and in
many instances the terminology of his pieces never allow us
to escape an awareness of the framework in which Eliot's
doctrinal and ethical preoccupations are set. For some this is
a matter for regret, for others one for rejoicing, yet whether
our inclination is to reject or embrace the Christian viewpoint,
we should be cautious not to allow our attitude to sway our
critical judgement of Eliot's plays as literature or as drama.
We do not need to endorse with our personal approval an
author's opinions or convictions in order to appreciate the
skill with which they are demonstrated or expounded.

Yet there are undoubted problems to be faced in dealing
with such works as *Murder in the Cathedral* and *The Cocktail
Party*. In the case of the former Eliot himself admits in his
lecture on *Poetry and Drama* (1951):

> I had the advantage for a beginner, of an occasion which called
> for a subject generally admitted to be suitable for verse . . . my
> play was to be produced for a rather special kind of audience –
> an audience of those serious people who go to 'festivals' and
> expect to have to put up with poetry . . . it was a religious play,
> and people who go deliberately to a religious play at a religious
> festival expect to be patiently bored and to satisfy themselves
> with the feeling that they have done something meritorious. . . .
> (*On Poetry and Poets*, p. 79)

What he omits to say is that a large percentage of those who
first saw the play at Canterbury would have felt reasonably
at home with many of its attitudes and much of its biblically-
inspired language, *because* they were practising Christians.
The action included liturgical chants towards which at least
High Church Anglicans were orientated; the acts were

separated from each other by the comfortably recognisable device of a sermon; the central martyrdom of Becket was led up to in a manner not unlike that in which the Mass or Holy Communion service paves the way to the act of reception. Above all, the play incorporated choric speeches which, however careful their author was to maintain a neutrality of tone, came at times very close to recalling the characteristic cadences of the Bible and the imagery of Anglican worship. Moments of theatre the piece undoubtedly contained – most notably perhaps Becket's encounter with the unexpected Fourth Tempter – but many of them depended in a larger measure than is sometimes acknowledged upon the assumption among early audiences of a certain familiarity with Christian concepts and modes of utterance. Eliot in *Murder in the Cathedral* had the enormous advantage initially of preaching to the converted, and his play in its first presentation was not far from being an act of worship.

As the piece reached a wider audience, both in the playhouse and in the printed text, as it no longer enjoyed the advantages derived from production in the semi-ecclesiastical environment of a cathedral chapter house, with all its wealth of associations, architectual, historical and theological, its overt Christianity became a stumbling-block for many non-believers still capable of responding positively to music or painting of Christian provenance. Eliot was felt by some to have too palpable a design on his audiences, to be guilty of some religious confidence trick. It is therefore especially important to analyse the 'Christian dimension' in Eliot's plays carefully, in order to assess just how dependent they are for their total impact on matters of orthodox religious belief.

It has been frequently observed that the Chorus in *Murder in the Cathedral*, the Women of Canterbury 'forced to bear witness' to the trauma of Becket's martyrdom, serve as the spectators' proxies in the action of the drama, and it is notable that Eliot is therefore at pains to depict them not as devout neophytes or even convinced believers, but rather as *femmes moyen sensuelles*, weak in their faith, human in their fears and reluctant to become 'involved'. It is implied that these are they for whom the martyrs and saints who lay down their lives set an example and strengthen belief, much as Christians believe that Christ died in order to save the human race from spiritual death. The doctrinal significance of the role of the Women lies in their initial anxiety to avert what they view at the outset as a potential disaster, the pointless stirring-up of hostility occasioned by the Archbishop's return to Canterbury, which can only terminate in a painful scene of wanton slaughter to which they will be compelled through cowardice to assent. Their wish is to be spared the proximity of death:

> O Thomas our Lord, leave us and leave us be, in our humble
> and tarnished frame of existence, leave us; do not ask us
> To stand to the doom on the house, the doom on the Archbishop,
> the doom on the world. [p. 244]

During the course of the play the Women come to learn the function of evil in God's universe and the purposes of Christian martyrdom; just as Becket in addressing the audience at the end of Part 1 draws a distinction between 'senseless self-sacrifice' and the calm acceptance of God's will, so the Women have to attain to a state wherein they can acquiesce in the Archbishop's murder, knowing that in the words of his sermon:

> A martyrdom is always the design of God, for His love of men, to
> warn them and to lead them, to bring them back to His ways.
> [p. 261]

The Women reach such a measure of understanding by acknowledging their share as human beings in the general guilt and corruption of mankind, in a pit of cosmic foulness from which only such redemptive acts as Christ's and Becket's can ultimately save them. The final triumphant chorus of praise which concludes Part II is testimony to the enhanced sense of vision bestowed on 'the poor women of Canterbury', even though they still have to admit that they themselves are not the stuff of which martyrs are made:

We thank Thee for Thy mercies of blood, for Thy redemption
  by blood. For the blood of Thy martyrs and saints
Shall enrich the earth, shall create the holy places.   [p. 281]

The doctrinal function of Becket himself is more
sophisticated, as befits the character whose role comes closest
to that of the tragic protagonist of a secular type of drama. It
is he who in traditional terms carries the 'message' of Eliot's
play, both as representative human victim of state oppression
and as archetypal Christian martyr and saint. The piece is in
some measure a defence of Becket and a justification of the
Church's attitude to martyrdom, addressed implicitly,
perhaps, at sceptics who might wish to question Becket's
motives or seek to challenge the spiritual value of what to
outsiders could appear to be an unnecessary death.
    From his first entry Becket behaves as someone who is
prepared to die in order to maintain the authority of the
Church against that of the Crown in certain key matters –

Loathing power given by temporal devolution,
Wishing subjection to God alone   [p. 242]

– aware that 'End will be simple, sudden, God-given'. What
he does not foresee – and this forms the crisis of Part I – is
that his own motives for laying himself open to martyrdom
may be those of a proud man seeking glory for himself rather
than seeking to do the will of God. Resisting with little
difficulty those Tempters who offer him the resumption of a
life of sensual pleasure, worldly power in the opportunity to
combine the offices of Archbishop and the Chancellor of
England and the chance to join a coalition of interests against
the King, Becket has not reckoned to receive a fourth visitor
who offers the most insidious temptation, not only that 'of
glory after death' when as saint and martyr he will 'rule from
the tomb', but also the 'heavenly grandeur' of the saintly
crown reserved for those who die in God's service. He is
temporarily shaken by this graphic presentation of his own
suppressed aspirations, but his agony of spirit, though
obscured in terms of the play's visible action, culminates in

the triumphant speech which concludes the first part of the play:

> Now is my way clear, now is the meaning plain:
> Temptation shall not come in this kind again.   [p. 258]

As he remarks in his Christmas sermon, 'the true martyr is he who has become the instrument of God, who has lost his will in the will of God, and who no longer deserves anything for himself, not even the glory of being a martyr' [p. 261].

Becket's mental torment is over; his physical ordeal is about to begin. In Part II, although he defends his past conduct vigorously before the Knights, he is clearly ready for the end, accepting that

> Death will come only when I am worthy,
> And if I am worthy, there is no danger.   [p. 271]

He acknowledges that in the eyes of a world which argues from results, his reluctance to save himself will appear fanatical and feckless, but in terms of his religious beliefs he sees himself as justified:

> We have only to conquer
> Now, by suffering.   [p. 274]

Vindicated in death, Thomas has testified to the strength of the Church and the God whom it seeks to serve, and the Third and most farsighted of the Priests voices the argument for the apparent paradox of the hymn of praise which backs the final chorus:

> Let our thanks ascend
> To God, who has given us another Saint in Canterbury.
>   [p. 281]

It is thus virtually impossible to detach *Murder in the Cathedral* from the doctrinal shell in which it is encased; the play is steeped in explicitly expressed Christian notions of sin

and atonement, self-abnegation and obedience to God and
the ultimate unimportance of temporal values by comparison
with transcendental ones. Though it would be false to suggest
that the play lacks any focus other than the doctrinal, it must
depend for its full appreciation on some knowledge and
understanding of the Christian scale of values, of religious
references and of the nature of the beliefs it embodies. On
this occasion Eliot had no inhibitions about making his
allegiances plain. But by the time he came to write *The
Family Reunion* for performance in 1939, and *The Cocktail Party*
for the Edinburgh Festival of 1949, he had accepted that to
make his plays palatable in the very different milieu of the
commercial theatre he would need to provide his religious
pill with a secular coating. (One question we shall need to
ask later is how far the coating impeded the efficacy of the
pill.)

Just as *The Family Reunion* seeks to deal with issues
concerning guilt and expiation in terms of ancestral legacies
and family secrets (thus proclaiming itself in some measure
the heir of the naturalistic tradition of Ibsen and his
successors), so *The Cocktail Party* cloaks its didactic purposes
by pretending on the surface to be one of those comedies of
social and sexual manners all too prevalent on the English
commercial stage in the '30s and '40s. Yet although Eliot has
now jettisoned the overt use of the customary accompaniments
of divine worship, of which he made unashamed dramatic
capital in *Murder in the Cathedral*, *The Cocktail Party* can still be
recognised as a thinly veiled doctrinal parable illustrating the
Christian faith's perennial concern with sin and forgiveness,
with personal conduct and redemption, but with its incidents
and figures drawn from contemporary life, albeit from a
rather unrepresentative social stratum, namely the affluent
and influential professional classes, whose behaviour, doings
and lifestyle obsessed playwrights at the period when Eliot
was attempting to have his Wooden Horse dragged into the
citadel of the West End.

The Cocktail Party is slow to declare its serious aims; early
in I i the party gossip and badinage are fully sustained, the
only 'deeper' strand being the dual mystery of Lavinia's

absence and the presence of the 'Unidentified Guest', and
even the former is explained in quite naturalistic terms when
Edward is alone with his interlocutor. Moreover, Reilly's
diagnosis of his host's *malaise* is expressed in the language of
the psychiatrist's couch rather than the confessional. The
first hint of anything of more spiritual relevance perhaps
comes with Peter's allusion to the 'tranquillity' which he
senses Celia's company creates, although this is lost sight of
in the quasi-farcical goings and comings, and in the knowledge
that she has been having an adulterous affair with Edward.
However, Edward's discovery that he wants Lavinia back,
and Celia's realisation that she and her lover have been
living in a realm of illusion, are often formulated in rather
different terms from those customarily employed in plays
which depend on marital infidelity and sexual permutations
for their staple appeal:

> I see that my life was determined long ago
> And that this struggle to escape from it
> Is only a make-believe, a pretence
> That what is, is not, or could be changed.   [p. 381]

Even so, it is noticeable that even Eliot cannot prevent the
language sliding into the trite clichés of 'romance' on
occasion:

> I suppose that most women
> Would feel degraded to find that a man
> With whom they thought they had shared something wonderful
> Had taken them only as a passing diversion.   [p. 380]

The climax of I ii is Edward's acknowledgement of the
middle-aged mediocrity he is doomed to come to terms with
and Celia's admission that she has been seeking a spiritual
satisfaction that Edward cannot give her; the rest of the play
is the history of the implications of these discoveries, a quest
which Reilly initiates in I iii, by offering to repair the
Chamberlaynes' rickety marriage by getting them to face the
truth about their relationship, the necessity for which the

long bickering duologue which concludes the scene makes
obvious. By the end Edward's diction in particular alerts the
listener or reader to the theological dimension in the situation,
which helps it to transcend any merely local and personal
interest it may possess:

> What is hell? Hell is oneself . . .
> > It was only yesterday
> That damnation took place . . .
> What devil left the door on the latch
> For these doubts to enter? And then you came back, you
> The angel of destruction . . .   [pp. 397–8]

  Act Two is devoted to Reilly's 'redemption' from ruin of the
lives of Edward and Lavinia by persuading them that what
they are inclined to regard as an intolerable arrangement is
in fact bearable if they are only prepared to accept that it is
their common faults and inadequacies which can bind
together

> A man who finds himself incapable of loving
> And a woman who finds no man can love her. [p. 410]

Reilly's advice that they should work out their 'salvation
with diligence' is phrased so that it prefigures the very
different form of vocation which is to be Celia's:

> The best of a bad job is all any of us make of it –
> Except of course, the saints . . .   [p. 410]

  The Chamberlaynes can learn to bear the burdens on their
consciences in the give-and-take of daily living, but Celia has
a different destiny; for her as for Becket there is a more
awesome but more glorious fate appointed. Her experience
with Edward has led her to feel not only that they were
simply using each other, but that the world of personal
relationships and 'ordinary' domestic life is a delusion, that
she is alone with 'a sense of sin' that she feels she must atone
for, not in the sense of making amends to anyone (least of all
Lavinia), but by choosing a way of life which will fulfill her

deepest spiritual needs more absolutely than the affair with
Edward ever did or could do. As she herself says:

> You see, I think I really had a vision of something
> Though I don't know what it is. I don't want to forget it.
> I want to live with it. I could do without everything,
> Put up with anything, if I might cherish it.   [p. 418]

Reilly guides Celia then towards her ultimate goal, which
like Becket's turns out to be a violent death in the service of
others: Eliot is scrupulous not to use the terminology of the
Christian religion, but Celia's death 'crucified/Very near an
ant-hill' has to be seen as analogous to that of a martyr of
the Church, and possibly Reilly's sentence summoning the
Guardians after the consultations are ended acts as a further
pointer to those initiated enough in the Gospels to know that
'It is finished' were Christ's final words from the cross. Yet
Eliot offsets this with the quasi-pagan libation – the one
moment of serious stylisation in the entire play – and this
warns us to avoid too exclusively orthodox an interpretation
of Celia's fate.
    The final act resorts to the more inconsequential exchanges
of i i, although we are now in a position to see the characters
with keener eyes, and the increased integration between
Edward and Lavinia as married partners is plain to see and
hear. Knowing the spiritual authority Alex and Julia bear,
even the farcical traveller's tale of the monkey-eating
Christians of Kinkanja seems introduced for a purpose, as we
eventually discover with the shattering news of Celia's horrific
murder. But by now the figure most in need of 'salvation' is
Peter Quilpe who has been 'living on' an image of Celia,
much as she and Edward during their love-affair fabricated
phoney images of each other to feed their own egos. Celia by
breaking free found her happiness in accepting, as did Becket,
a role in the overall design which was to lead to her death –

> And if that is not a happy death, what death is happy?
>   [p. 437]

The nature of her death, again like Becket's, proved that her life was far from purposeless or wasted. The problems with which *The Cocktail Party* concludes is for the others, the survivors, to convert the memories of their behaviour towards Celia into something positive; meanwhile the Chamberlaynes must accept the consequences of their choice and shoulder, as their 'appointed burden', making a success of their latest cocktail party.

Spiritually speaking, *The Cocktail Party* is far less esoteric and exclusive than *Murder in the Cathedral*, which largely concentrates on the arguments in justification of Christian martyrdom and on the gulf between the saint chosen of God and the lay public forced to bear witness. Although it has its own saint who suffers death in following the demands of her own vision, *The Cocktail Party* gives even greater prominence to those who 'maintain themselves by the common routine' and carries the message that God's purposes may be equally well served by those who reconcile themselves to the human condition by accepting its limitations and its disappointments and sharing with a fellow creature the sense of failure that this entails. What both plays have in common is the fundamental conviction that there is a God, and that he has a purpose which it is the business of the human race to discover and attempt to fulfill according to our abilities. The chief difference is that Eliot's later play announces its religious position far more flexibly and far less stridently than its predecessor. But as we shall see, neither piece depends for its *total* impact on its doctrinal function.

3   DRAMA AND RITUAL

In a discussion found under the heading 'Dramatis Personae' in the *Criterion* magazine for April 1923 Eliot wrote that 'the failure of the contemporary stage to satisfy the craving for ritual is one of the reasons why it is not a living art'. Like his

Irish contemporary W. B. Yeats, Eliot put his faith in forms
of ceremonial and hierarchic systems to restore order and
purpose to many twentieth-century political and cultural
organisms, and in the case of the modern drama which he
viewed as simply content to mirror the most superficial and
ephemeral aspects of contemporary life instead of transcending
them, some attempt to return to the ancient preoccupations
of the theatre seemed vital. Moreover, for a playwright not
committed to a naturalistic style of presentation, ritual and
dramatic conventions of a non-realistic nature would enable
a number of intractable problems to be solved. Ritual can
allow overt comment of a philosophical or moralistic kind to
be introduced in a manner which would break the veneer of
credibility in a naturalistic play: the Chorus in a Greek
tragedy or the Prologue of an Elizabethan drama permits the
authorial voice or at any rate that of a commentator standing
outside the action to be heard. Moreover, the presence of
ritualistic elements can help to highlight what is of more
than passing importance and temporal validity in drama,
creating that essential process by which what is extraneous
and redundant is transcended, so that a sense of universal
relevance is achieved, even if in the short term total credibility
is lost. Finally, the role of ritual can often be to link drama
with its origins in acts of religious worship, whether they be
primitive rites or the ceremonies of the early Church.

Yeats found his models for what he sought to do in the
theatre in some of the conventions of the Japanese Noh stage
of the Middle Ages, which included the employment of a
chorus and musicians present on stage, the wearing of masks
by the chief actors, highly-stylised performance techniques
and a prescribed structural and narrative pattern to the
texts. Eliot in his turn discovered the devices he felt to be
needful in the sacred routines and liturgy of the Christian
Church, in the formal characteristics of the ancient Greek
stage, particularly the central part played by the Chorus,
and occasionally in the accepted traditions of popular
entertainment, although these are less obviously in evidence
in *Murder in the Cathedral* and *The Cocktail Party* than in *Sweeney
Agonistes* and *The Rock*.

In composing *Murder in the Cathedral* Eliot could be reasonably sure that in the main he would be catering for the tastes of a fairly select clientèle, who would be accustomed on the whole to the formulae and rites of Anglican church worship. In *The Rock* he had felt free to employ the patterns of supplication and praise which had shaped the Christian liturgy from its earliest days, often utilising the typical parallelism of Hebrew prosody, whereby one statement is offset or echoed by another, or the device of patterned repetition, one of the stock features of worship all over the globe. In the smaller auditorium of Canterbury Cathedral's chapter house he was able to develop and refine his technique to suit a more sanctified occasion, but the role of ritual remained paramount.

The most obvious means by which ritual makes its presence known in *Murder in the Cathedral* is through the constantly employed device of the Chorus of poor women, about whose introductory lines there is something already vaguely ceremonial:

Here let us stand, close by the cathedral. Here let us wait.

[p. 239]

The Women assembling to witness a spectacle that they only sense is about to occur heightens the formal aspect of the drama, which the non-naturalistic mode of choral delivery, with its description of the sequence of seasonal keynotes and its rhetorical pattern of verbal repetition helps to enhance. The Women are participants in a rite whose significance they do not yet comprehend.

The priests who appear next are given individualised personalities, so that although they speak in formal sequence, their roles at this stage are more naturalistically conceived than those of the Women, and the encounter with the know-all Messenger is conducted at the play's most domesticated level. However, their contrasting comments after the Messenger's departure revive the tone of the choruses, and the Third Priest no longer speaks in character so much as adopts the stance of impartial commentator on the action as often is the case in Greek tragedy, when he invokes the play's leading image of the wheel and draws directly on the graphic imagery of the Bible (*Ecclesiastes* XII. 3–4):

> For good or ill, let the wheel turn.
> The wheel has been still, these seven years, and no good.
> For ill or good, let the wheel turn.
> For who knows the end of good or evil?
> Until the grinders cease
> And the door shall be shut in the street,
> And all the daughters of music shall be brought low.

[p. 243]

The chorus which follows is a fine blend of specific image and general statement: there is a strong flavour of ritual diction in the constant repetitions – 'late late late' and 'grey grey grey' and the haunting refrain 'Living and partly living' – and in the cumulative phrasing of such lines as

> A doom on the house, a doom on yourself, a doom on the world.

[p. 243]

The exchanges between Thomas and the Priests are again couched in more naturalistic vein, and the successive visitations of the Tempters, while obeying the formal pattern met with a medieval play such as *Everyman* to which Eliot acknowledged a debt, are handled in a variety of rhetorical manners, the most obvious set of ritual utterances coming in the Archbishop's brief bout with the Second Tempter:

THOMAS: Who shall have it?
TEMPTER: He who will come.
THOMAS: What shall be the month?
TEMPTER: The last from the first.
THOMAS: What shall we give for it?
TEMPTER: Pretence of priestly power.
THOMAS: Why should we give it?
TEMPTER: For the power and the glory.
THOMAS: No!

[p. 249]

But the most heavily ritualised passages come at the culmination of the 'Temptation Scene' where the Women, the Tempters and the Priests take turns to express their responses to Becket's final dilemma, and then speak lines alternately, their images connected in threes, and their rhetorical structures often identical. Here Eliot makes the fullest use possible of the advantages of freedom from strict realism: Becket is at the heart of some all-involving rite of which he is both celebrant and victim.

Part II features more liturgical ritual than the first part; in the first production the opening chorus which now appears in the printed text was left out, so that the three processions with their interspersed introits set the action on its way. It was a simple but effective means of handling time in the play, although few would strictly be concerned about such matters; more probably Eliot introduced the liturgical element in order to pave the way for his 'Grand Finale', the final chorus based on the angelic hymn *'Gloria in excelsis'* which Becket also takes as the text for his sermon on Christmas morning. The presence of the banners of the saints displayed in sequence is also of dramatic value in that the arrival of the Knights to kill Becket is the cue for these images of other-worldly concerns to be removed from view.

The encounter with the Knights contains little of a formalised nature, but every now and then Eliot reminds his audience that the action is not strictly lifelike; the Knights speak and sing in chorus, or their lines take on a cumulative force as in:

FIRST KNIGHT: Priest, you have spoken in peril of your
                    life.
SECOND KNIGHT: Priest, you have spoken in danger of the
                    knife.
THIRD KNIGHT: Priest, you have spoken treachery and
                    treason.
THE THREE KNIGHTS: Priest! traitor, confirmed in malfeasance.
                                                      [p. 269]

There is a ritual dimension to Becket's murder (which was mimed iconographically in the original production): the background of the *Dies Irae* as the Priests drag him to the cathedral and of the *Te Deum* for the last chorus cannot help but give the play the air of a religious rite, an impression reinforced by the impassioned chorus which accompanies the killing. This sense is immeasurably increased when the Four Knights step out of the picture frame as it were to deliver their 'modern-dress' *apologiae* and in doing so accentuate the sacramental nature of what we have just witnessed. The four liturgical petitions which conclude the play are a final reminder of just how dependent on ritual formulations *Murder in the Cathedral* is.

In Eliot's plays written for the commercial stage such formulae and routines are more cautiously disguised, as the dramatist's declared aims demanded. In *The Family Reunion* he was naturally compelled to reproduce the superficial aspects of the standard West End vehicle with titled personages, drinks on a tray, gibes at the young and the *parvenus*, with attendant butlers and chauffeurs to give the piece 'class'. But having lulled his audiences into a state of false security, the playwright could still use ritual modes to point up his covert themes.

One obvious way in which *The Family Reunion* does this is to replace the overt deployment of a chorus by requiring one group of characters to submerge their individual roles as Amy's eccentric relations into a choric function, by which means they can comment on the action as it unfolds. As a result they can in theory fulfill a dual purpose, witnessing the events of the play as both participants and more neutral observers. Such a device has the effect of suspending the naturalistic action while the Chorus communes with itself and the audience, so that some may feel the play proceeds by fits and starts, but it does assist spectators to accept the dimension of ritual when it is required to function, as for instance in Part I Scene II when the hero and heroine share a lyrical love-duet which Eliot came later to find unjustified dramatically speaking as extraneous to the situation, or in Agatha's speech of propitiation which concludes the first part. But the most striking piece of ritual comes at the end of the play when the heroine and the most farsighted of the

relations perform a ceremony with the hero's mother's
birthday cake as its centrepiece:

> AGATHA *and* MARY *walk slowly in single file round and round the*
> *table, clockwise. At each revolution they blow out a few candles, so that*
> *their last words are spoken in the dark.*   [p. 349]

Exciting as Eliot's attempts to incorporate such devices
into the everyday texture of *The Family Reunion* were, he
himself had severe doubts as to the wisdom of trying to
combine techniques from a non-naturalistic mode of theatre
into a play which was strenuously attempting to mirror the
dominant dramatic style of its period. For one thing the
awkward transitions involved in the transformation of the
minor characters into choric figures were too taxing for both
audiences and players to be entirely successful; personages in
whose truth to life one was invited to believe at one moment
suddenly took on an extra, non-realistic, collective identity,
though without the superior insight usually accorded to a
Greek chorus.

Thus it is that in *The Cocktail Party* Eliot dispensed with the
chorus in both its disguised and its overt form; in one way
this is a further concession to the potency of the naturalistic
play of everyday life, governed by what W. H. Auden had
spoken of as 'sad sour Probability', yet it was inevitable
given the problem of dovetailing elements taken from the
world of ritualistic practice into plays concerned at least on
one level with the realm of the mundane. But Eliot did not
abandon ritual from *The Cocktail Party* completely although
the only occasion on which ceremonial is consciously invoked
is in the 'libation scene' at the end of Act Two, when Reilly,
Julia and Alex toast the Chamberlaynes and Celia as they
'build the hearth' and 'go upon a journey' respectively. Here
the language is deliberately incantatory, although as we have
seen curiously devoid of traditional Christian symbolism:

> Watch over her in the desert.
> Watch over her in the mountain.
> Watch over her in the labyrinth.
> Watch over her by the quicksand.   [p. 422]

But there is another aspect of ritual in *The Cocktail Party* which tends to get forgotten, although it is admittedly of a rather different order from those discussed so far. But in so far as it helps to create a dimension to the play which takes it beyond the drab, mimetic photographic realism to which so much contemporary drama was committed in 1949, it is worth selecting for comment. Eliot is very alert to the rituals of social behaviour, and the comedy is often achieved as a result of techniques which go back to *Sweeney Agonistes* and a path the author chose not to explore very far. But trite exchanges like the following have an important part to play in the ritual content of *The Cocktail Party*:

CELIA: She's such a good mimic.
JULIA: Am I a good mimic?
PETER: You *are* a good mimic. You never miss anything.
[p. 354]

The same compliment might be paid to Eliot:

JULIA: I feel as if I knew
        All about that aunt in Hampshire.
EDWARD: Hampshire?
JULIA: Didn't you say Hampshire?
EDWARD: No, I didn't say Hampshire.
JULIA: Did you say Hampstead?
EDWARD: No, I didn't say Hampstead.
JULIA: But she must live somewhere.
EDWARD: She lives in Essex.
JULIA: Anywhere near Colchester? Lavinia loves oysters.
[p. 357]

Eliot's rituals can sometimes prove highly entertaining ones.

4   Drama and Realism

As we have already seen, for practically the whole of Eliot's lifetime the Western European theatre was under the influence of dramatic naturalism, an influence he associated with the prevalence of prose drama, perhaps his most sustained comment on the issue being put in the mouth of one of the speakers in his 'Dialogue on Dramatic Poetry' (1928):

> People have tended to think of verse as a restriction upon drama
> . . . [and that] Only prose can give the full gamut of modern
> feeling, can correspond to actuality. But . . . are we not merely
> deceiving ourselves when we aim at greater and greater realism?
> Are we not contenting ourselves with appearances, instead of
> insisting upon fundamentals? . . . I say that prose drama is
> merely a slight by-product of verse drama. The human soul, in
> intense emotion, strives to express itself in verse. It is not for me,
> but for the neurologists, to discover why this is so, and why and
> how feeling and rhythm are related. The tendency, at any rate,
> of prose drama is to emphasise the ephemeral and superficial; if
> we want to get at the permanent and universal we tend to
> express ourselves in verse.   (*Selected Essays*, p. 46)

It has often been argued that Eliot's speaker is here making an arbitrary and artificial distinction between prose and verse; like Yeats, he is taking a deliberately limited view of the use of dramatic prose, confining its role to discussing topics of only temporary social or moral concern, forgetting that prose drama can also handle questions of perennial human relevance reaching far beyond 'the ephemeral and superficial'. Moreover, prose, in the hands of a master craftsman such as Synge, Beckett or Pinter, can clearly transcend its apparent relationship with 'actuality' and create an emotional atmosphere every bit as charged with feeling as that achieved by verse. Even the common phrases and clichés of contemporary life may become transmuted into effective theatrical diction, as Eliot himself was able to demonstrate in *Sweeney Agonistes*.

We must therefore approach Eliot's plays in full knowledge

that he was attempting to challenge the dominant form of drama in his day, and that his pronouncements on the naturalistic prose play of modern life are not to be regarded as absolute judgements, any more than his strictures on Milton or the Georgian poets can be detached from what he was trying to achieve with his own poetic revolution. It is important, however, to examine the ways in which Eliot strove to break away from the accepted conventions of drama in the years between roughly 1900 and 1950, namely those established by Ibsen and his disciples or by such writers as Shaw, Galsworthy and Granville-Barker on one hand, and by such authors of social comedies as Oscar Wilde, Somerset Maugham, Frederick Lonsdale and Noel Coward.

Eliot certainly appears to have had little time for the dramatic achievements of any of these playwrights, although it is quite clear from his own theatrical efforts following *Murder in the Cathedral* that he was well aware of the components of the so-called 'Problem Play' pioneered in the late nineteenth century, which usually involved dealing with sexual intrigue and questions of personal ethics among the upper classes. It is also evident that when he set out to smuggle poetry and religion onto the West End stage, he was *au fait* with the kind of conventions which governed the light comedies that offered the general public access to the goings-on of the 'smart set' with their rich aunts and country cottages and concert-going and house parties. But his plays never evince any concern for social or political reform, which constituted a major part of the platform on which so many early twentieth-century playwrights (following Ibsen) took a stand. At the same time it is apparent that Eliot was not entirely indifferent to the importance of advocating ideas which went beyond the necessity for the individual to seek out his or her personal salvation. In *Murder in the Cathedral* in particular, Eliot is careful to avoid a purely historical approach to the conflict between Becket and Henry II, but he is skilful enough to weave into his narrative sufficient references for us to recognise the presence of a political and constitutional theme which had a great deal of relevance to Europe in 1935.

Few dramatists confronted with the subject of Becket and his martyrdom would be able to resist the introduction of Henry II into the action; their initial friendship and identity of interests, and their fatal clash on Becket's assumption of the archbishopric, is the stuff of which drama is normally made, and both Tennyson and Jean Anouilh in their versions of the story fully exploited its potential. But Eliot chose to focus on a single protagonist, allowing others to represent the forces of the secular power, and to have such background as he felt needful sketched in by the Chorus, the Priests and Becket himself. By doing this, he achieved a greater intensity of mood, and was able to divert attention from the intriguing figure of the King, in order to give the Archbishop pride of place.

But although the primary focus is on the nature of sainthood and the Christian value of martyrdom, *Murder in the Cathedral* is partly a study in political realities, albeit seen exclusively from the viewpoint of an individual conscience. But in the 1930s, with Germany, Italy, Russia and Turkey under virtually totalitarian regimes, and the Spanish Civil War on the verge of breaking out, Becket's defence of the Church against secular interference was of poignant interest to those who came to witness his defiant stand, aware that Churchmen both had been and would in the future be called on to make the same kind of sacrifice for their beliefs. While many of Eliot's contemporaries were prepared to believe that the State was supreme, *Murder in the Cathedral* was a declaration that there were certain areas over which the State had no jurisdiction.

There can be no mistaking that this desire to bring home the contemporary relevance of his presentation was what inspired Eliot to introduce the famous 'alienation effect' of having the Knights address the audience in prose speeches whose irony is beautifully controlled to demonstrate just how contemporary politicians set about justifying the unjustifiable. Each is skilfully arranged to mirror the temperament assigned to the Four Tempters of Part I (in the original production the parts were doubled), and the dramatist is able to parody exactly the tone of the upper-class English gentleman with all its pompousness and spurious appeals to good form and commonsense. The satire is broad but extremely telling:

> The fact is that we knew we had taken on a pretty stiff job; I'll only speak for myself, but I had drunk a good deal – I am not a drinking man ordinarily – to brace myself up for it. When you come to the point, it does go against the grain to kill an Archbishop, especially when you have been brought up in good Church traditions.

This is not precisely the language of the dictators, but the kinds of reasons which the Tempters adduce for the necessity of eliminating an undesirable element are analogous to those by which state suppression has been justified for much of this century. And there can be no mistaking the veiled threat in the First Knight's final 'suggestion':

> I think that there is no more to be said; and I suggest that you now disperse quietly to your homes. Please be careful not to loiter in groups at street corners, and do nothing that might provoke any public outbreak. [p. 280]

While it is notable that Eliot has recourse to the despised medium of prose here, it is a fact that by using it, he achieves both topicality and universality, in the suggestion that the strife between Becket and Henry II is only one phase in a battle which has to be fought in every generation. Past and present enter a dynamic relationship.

Another device which permits Eliot to transcend the immediacy of the present day without necessarily sacrificing relevance for a contemporary audience is through the use of myth as exemplified in the great tragedies of classical Greece. While this was one aspect of the dramatic form which appealed to Eliot, as we have already noted, it was only with the pieces intended for commercial consumption that he attempted to make direct analogies between his dramas and those of the ancient world. In *The Family Reunion* he actually introduces into the cast the Eumenides or Kindly Ones from the third part of Aeschylus's dramatic trilogy, the *Oresteia*, whose function is to hunt down the young Orestes for the murder of his mother and her lover. Harry Monchensey, Eliot's hero, is a modern Orestes, haunted by the fear that he may have murdered his wife; to him the Eumenides are real, but Eliot, instead of seeking out some modern equivalent, presents them as actual figures on stage, an effect he later came to believe to have been misguided. But its introduction was one of several devices for transcending the everyday reality in which plays of the genre which *The Family Reunion* superficially resembled usually specialised.

For *The Cocktail Party* Eliot relied on the myth embodied in a play by Euripides entitled *Alcestis* to provide his 'extra dimension'; in this tragicomedy Admetus, king of Pherae, has been promised reprieve from death if someone will die in his place: his wife Alcestis volunteers and is carried off to Hades. The hero Heracles (Hercules) shortly arrives and is entertained liberally enough to get drunk. Only then does he realise that Admetus has been keeping the truth of his bereavement from him; in astonished gratitude he offers to retrieve Admetus's wife from Death and restore her to him, which he does. The parallel with the situation in Eliot's play is not exact: Lavinia has hardly died in Edward's place, an action of which Celia seems much more capable, nor are the complicated sexual permutations of the modern characters found in Euripides's more temperate narrative. But the sense of loss experienced by Edward on Lavinia's defection, the intervention of the gin-drinking guest who offers to restore her by bringing her back from an unknown country, even the ineffective attempt to cover up Lavinia's absence, all these things contribute to our perception (or at least the perception of those who know their Greek mythology) of a level of meaning which provides *The Cocktail Party* with an escape route from the reflection of 'the ephemeral and superficial' which works in unison with the Christian dimension.

On the other hand, there is a price to be paid in this and in Eliot's last two plays, *The Confidential Clerk* and *The Elder Statesman*, both of which were written in loose imitation of classical Greek models. In *The Cocktail Party* the analogies with *Alcestis* are felt to be both distracting and arbitrary;

there seems no real dramatic reason for Reilly becoming drunk and slightly abusive to Julia in I i, apart from Eliot's private wish to point the parallel with the joviality of Heracles in the house of grief in Euripides. The price seems too high, especially as many parts of Eliot's play are not found paralleled in the earlier one: a considerable number of effective reworkings of classical themes have enhanced the modern stage – Anouilh's *Antigone*, Sartre's *Les Mouches* and Giraudoux's *Amphitryon 38* – but there the parallels and contrasts seem more carefully worked out, the classical material and the modern more happily fused. Certainly Eliot felt this was the deepest flaw in *The Family Reunion*, but it scarcely seems much more successfully accomplished in *The Cocktail Party*.

Perhaps this is because Eliot is all too accomplished at creating a pastiche of the conventional West End play which aims at achieving in selective form 'truth to life'. His awareness of what made the lighter plays of Terence Rattigan and virtually all the work of Coward, Ben Travers and the other suppliers of entertaining farce so popular led him to make too many compromises with the spirit of naturalism which he denigrated in so much of his writing on dramatic theory. For all his efforts to glide imperceptibly from party chatter and marital misdemeanours to questions of spiritual destiny and personal salvation. Eliot's satirical flair and accurate ear for everyday banalities may have played him false, betraying him into providing the enemy with too many hostages. Increasingly, his plays became less and less distinguishable from the West End frothinesses they were intended to supplant. By abandoning some of the elements which made his pieces stand out from the herd – the overt use of a chorus, the employment of a verse medium which drew attention to itself and by the development of devices which were the stock-in-trade of conventional drama –

EDWARD: But it's only that dreadful old woman who mattered – I shouldn't have minded anyone else.
    [*The doorbell rings.* EDWARD *goes to the door, saying:*]

But she always turns up when she's least wanted.
[*Opens the door*]
Julia!   [p. 359]

– Eliot probably made too many concessions to the genre in which he was determined to work. As a result, tension is often set up between the realistic detail of the settings, the conversations, the living conditions of the characters, and the sincerely-argued case for the recognition of a plane of experience far beyond the material world of phone-calls and eggs from the refrigerator. The old bottles ruin the taste of the new wine; the dish runs away with the spoon.

5   DRAMA AND PERSONALITY

One of our customary expectations in reading or seeing a play is that it will offer us intimate insight into the lives of other human beings, providing knowledge of the ways in which they perceive the world, or relate to others, or see themselves. But this is by no means an obligatory ingredient in the dramatic pudding: it is not a feature, for example, of the scripts which have survived from the medieval period, of which the anonymous *Everyman* forms a good example. Here the eponymous hero is a representative type of worldly man, and his individual quirks of personality, his responses and reactions, are irrelevant to his role in the drama: we never find out what makes Everyman 'tick'. Similarly the plays of the Japanese Noh tradition, which had a profound influence on the theatrical theories of Yeats, contain little by way of 'psychological interest' as it is understood in the West. It is simply that their authors wish to present other insights for our consideration than those which arise from an interest in human personality.

Something of the same kind of self-denial may be found in the earliest of Eliot's compositions for the stage; *Sweeney*

Agonistes is too concerned with a state of mental and spiritual *ennui* to present its protagonists as individual case histories; *The Rock* uses its characters as spokespeople for a range of viewpoints, and is similarly unconcerned with 'character'. In *Murder in the Cathedral* the position is rather more complex, but it still remains true that Eliot's interest is less in Becket as a character whose primary fascination is as an idiosyncratic human being, but rather as a man coming to terms with his appointed task as a servant of God. One is tempted to adapt Eliot's celebrated dictum on poetry and make it apply to his assessment of Becket's religious faith as being 'not a turning loose of emotion, but an escape from emotion . . . not the expression of personality, but an escape from personality'.

On the other hand, it is virtually impossible not to endow Becket with certain traits of character which have a bearing on the interest which we take in the play at whose 'still centre' he stands. Even at this distance of time from the twelfth century we can glimpse something of the immense personal charisma that this redoubtable prelate possessed. Eliot may have felt his choice of subject determined by the nature of the Canterbury commission, but there was already in existence a well-known play on Becket by the Victorian Poet Laureate, Lord Alfred Tennyson, written in 1879 and staged with great panache and success in 1893 by Henry Irving, who perhaps owed his knighthood to it two years later. Tennyson's five-act tragedy was actually presented in a truncated version in the chapter house at Canterbury as part of the 1932 and 1933 Festivals, so that it can only be that something in the 'Becket story' captured Eliot's imagination, and made him decide to rethink the way in which it might be presented on the modern stage. Tennyson's treatment had included the rivalry between Becket and Henry II, but had woven a romantic thread into the historical tapestry by making Becket the improbable guardian to Fair Rosamund, the King's mistress who incurs the jealousy of Queen Eleanor. Henry's hostility towards his Archbishop is thus given a double motivation, Eleanor poisoning her husband's mind against him; when the Knights murder Becket, we are asked to believe that Rosamund is actually praying in another part of the cathedral, reaching the Archbishop before he breathes his last!

Eliot clearly had no intention of falsifying the extant records of Becket's career in this way; the facts in themselves were sufficiently fascinating, including as they did Becket's humble origins, his rise to fortune and influence, his change of direction on being elevated to the see of Canterbury, his defiance of his former friend and patron, Henry II, his flight into exile and his return to be put to death at his place of work on 29 December 1170. But the dramatist had no wish to write a lengthy chronicle of politics and intrigue, even if the space (both physical and temporal) allocated to him had permitted it. Seeing that the essence of good drama is concentration, Eliot chose to commence *in medias res* and to focus on the last month of Becket's life, telling as much of the history of the previous years as he felt it necessary for the audience to be apprised of. Few would disagree that this was a sensible decision, or that it works totally satisfactorily in the theatre; although it is surprising just how much information of a documentary kind is conveyed during the course of a relatively short play, the allusions are not always self-explanatory.

The historical Becket is an enigma, and Eliot chooses to paint a rather more idealised picture of the prelate than many historians would do. Thomas Carlyle called him 'a noisy egotist and hypocrite' and there seems little doubt that he was proud, ostentatious, tactless, vain, popular with the commons and virtually fearless. At first sight Eliot appears to restrict Becket's character to a single trait, and that a flattering one, but the play does serve to demonstrate some of the less appealing aspects of its protagonist's personality. Part I may be viewed as charting Becket's progress from a state of spiritual pride and superiority to one of grace in which he accepts the will of God. If we are inclined to regard Becket's triumph over the first three Tempters as a matter for approval, we should also note that a certain sense of smugness marks each one. The note of self-congratulation is never far below the surface:

> Shall I who ruled like an eagle over doves
> Now take the shape of a wolf among wolves?
> Pursue your treacheries as you have done before:
> No one shall say that I betrayed a king.   (p. 252)

The shock conveyed by the Fourth Tempter is that he sees into the heart of Becket as only an *alter ego* can: Becket's mental crisis arises from the exposure of his one particular weakness – spiritual pride, a quality which the historical evidence leads one to believe was quite marked in the man himself. When the Knights accuse Becket of a variety of crimes in Part II, we are able to accept that in temporal terms they may be correct, that Becket's conduct was not always as free from reproach as he claims, but at this stage in the proceedings, Eliot has helped us to see that in Christian terminology, Becket's faults as a man are irrelevant to his significance *sub specie aeternitatis*, that his mortal weaknesses are as nothing by comparison with his saintly strengths. But this of course carries less conviction than it might for many people, since we are accustomed to judging character on a material basis, rather than on a spiritual one.

Moreover, this need to be convinced as to Becket's qualities of sanctity is not supported from the text as well as might be: to witness a dramatic figure wrestling with his or her conscience is often a very intense and moving experience, as those who have seen a performance of *Macbeth* or *Phaedra* will willingly testify. But at the very key point in Becket's crisis of faith – when the Fourth Tempter has exposed him to his own unworthy ambition to seek martyrdom for the attendant glory it will bring – Eliot draws a curtain across the picture of Becket Agonistes. All we know is that Thomas's initial words have been turned back on him by the most cunning of the Tempters, that this is a moment of supreme importance for the powers of light and darkness, that there appears to be no point in striving to achieve since all achievement, however seemingly altruistic, is really self-seeking, that it might be best for Becket to abandon the struggle, that even God's guidance might be inadequate to sustain the quest. And then, amazingly, without explanation, Becket is released from the dark night of the soul and is confident once again. But what inner resources, what arguments, he drew on, whether it was the final pleas of the Women in Canterbury that reconciled him to the rightness of what he proposed, is never made clear. A more psychologically-orientated creator of dramatic characters might have articulated the inner battle more satisfactorily.

Undoubtedly by focusing in the main on Becket the saint and martyr rather than on the historical paradox or the tragic hero, Eliot gave himself problems in Part II, for Becket is essentially a passive participant in the action after the anguish he undergoes in Part I. His interest for the audience is likely to be diminished because he is now left with no doubts or qualms about his fate: he does not strike out against it but rather embraces it as part of God's overall design. If Part I shows Becket triumphing over himself and the temptations laid before him, Part II can legitimately only show him meekly accepting death at the hands of the Knights without demur. But it is obviously hard to raise much dramatic interest in a hero who passively accepts, even welcomes, death, as the French seventeenth-century playwright Corneille demonstrates in his neo-classical tragedy, *Polyeucte*, which also features a Christian martyr. Here the demands of the stage clash once again with the dictates of orthodox theology.

So, in order to create some sense of conflict, Eliot is forced to drag Thomas back into the temporal sphere for a time, and have him put up a more spirited defence of his previous conduct than might be considered entirely credible in a man who has made his peace with the world and his own destiny. This must be admitted to produce a pronounced sense of contradiction; Becket, having rejected the values and time scale of the temporal kingdom in favour of the heavenly region, is now seen using its standards and criteria to justify his behaviour, conduct which presumably in theological terms now means very little to him. The point is not that this line of proceeding is false to the historical truth – Eliot is in fact heavily indebted to the eye-witness account of Becket's death as recorded by his crucifer Edward Grim – but rather that the final impact of the Archbishop's surrender to the will of God is weakened by his vigorous resistance to the Knights' arguments.

It might be possible to rationalise this contradiction by suggesting that having made his peace with God, Becket can now return to more mundane concerns, knowing that what matters is not his role in the world below but in the world to come; it might be said that whereas Part I is concerned with the internal conflict Becket undergoes, Part II has to concentrate on the less spiritually significant but undeniable external conflict. Or it could be said that Part II is not really focused on Becket at all, but rather on the Women of Canterbury whose weakness and apathy have partly inspired the prelate to accept death in order to awaken them to the truth of the Christian message. But it serves to illustrate the difficulties Eliot faced in treating Becket's story as a subject for a drama which invites us to psychological speculation, but which ultimately requires us to dispense with it.

With *The Cocktail Party* matters are rather different because Eliot is now working within a stage convention which permits him to present characters as psychological types who although they may be motivated in part by concerns not normally the subject of dramatic treatment, are still presented in terms of their inner compulsions, their interpersonal relationships and all those aspects of personality with which we are all familiar. Celia may be a saint in the making, but she is also an attractive woman in fashionable society who goes to parties and the pictures and has feelings and thoughts with which we can usually identify. Admittedly, it is Edward who receives the fullest in-depth treatment as a character, but then this is partly because Celia's spiritual condition lies further outside the normal parameters of dramatic motivation and Eliot's interest in her condition lies beyond psychological exploration.

There is thus, on this level at least, a much more fruitful collaboration in *The Cocktail Party* between the requirements of naturalistic drama and the doctrinal concerns which Eliot wishes to focus on. Whereas in *The Family Reunion* we have seen the conflicts resulting from the chorus of relations being

obliged to serve a dual function, in the later play Eliot is free
to treat his characters naturalistically even when their
dramatic function is extended far beyond the conscious level
of experience. This can occasionally produce incongruous
effects, as for example at the close of the drinking of the
libation where Reilly remarks that there is one – Peter
Quilpe – 'for whom the words cannot be spoken' since he
'has not yet come to where the words are valid' to which
Julia replies 'Shall we ever speak them?' Alex's response is,
to say the least, devastatingly bathetic:

> Others, perhaps, will speak them.
> You know, I have connections – even in California.   (p. 423)

The elevated tone of the Guardians' language is suddenly
reduced to the level of stock comic characterisation, causing
a jolt almost as great as that which results from the choric
arias in *The Family Reunion*.

Generally speaking, though, it must be admitted that Eliot
handles the characterisation in *The Cocktail Party* successfully.
He captures the broad types of which Julia is the most
obvious example with economy and not a little wit; the
'scatty', domineering, warm-hearted party guest is credibly
irritating, yet never as maddeningly so as she would be in
real life. Alex too is well conceived as the globe-trotting man
who has 'the lot', the life-and-soul of the party, the hearty,
practical amateur cook who runs other people's lives as well
as his own. Lavinia too is well observed, quite lethal in her
way, far too clear-sighted and coolly mocking to be happily
married to Edward, alive to his failings and not unaware of
her own. Peter is a little thinly drawn, perhaps, but one
senses that his interest for Eliot exists largely in embryo; his
trial is perhaps to come. At the same time it is apparent that
he is really required to act as Lavinia's illicit partner and so
act as a male counterpart to Celia; he too needs to seek out a
pattern for his future existence in the knowledge that Celia
was a very different person from what he had imagined for
himself.

But perhaps Eliot's finest success is with Edward whose

ordeal is presented in close-up in much the same way as Becket's is. His discomfiture at Lavinia's absence from the party, his efforts to cover up, his resentment at Reilly's interference, his realisation that he no longer wants Celia, his admission that he needs to take stock of his life, is all quite neatly conveyed to us. Even his self-pity in his despair rings true; self-centred and incapable of loving, his lack of pleasure on seeing both Celia and Lavinia unexpectedly is typical of him. But he is right to feel resentful of the way Lavinia organises his life and her air of superiority; it may be said that they deserve each other. Only Reilly can reveal their mutual suitability, even if it is expressed in negative terms, and their route to mutual tolerance, though not charted with any great precision, is plausible.

The final character is Celia, of whom something has already been said. She is not an easy figure to make credible, if only because her rarity as a human specimen is all too apparent. She does have a life in the real world, though here again the social exclusiveness of the shared London flat and the parents with an ancestral mansion in the country, her poetry and her interest in cinema, make her contact with the nitty-gritty of life rather tenuous. But her spiritual destiny can have the effect of depersonalising her, rather as Becket is isolated from those around him, and to an even more pronounced extent, Harry Monchensey. These people can all seem a little cold and lacking in what we normally regard as personality, almost as if they had been conceived in the head rather than the heart to illustrate a doctrinal point rather than to show how people behave. Part of the problem is that we do not see Celia in action after her 'conversion' as we do Lavinia and Edward; if one compares Shaw's character of St Joan one realises how much easier it is to portray even sanctity if it is given something to do. Celia among the sick natives of Kinkanja would doubtless be somebody to whom we could respond. That is perhaps why Eliot was wise to couple the story of Celia Coplestone with that of Edward and Lavinia Chamberlayne, and this is a measure of his expanded interest in the plight of individuals *unlike* Becket, Harry and Celia, who are not called upon to embrace the way of suffering.

6   Drama and Poetry

Eliot's motives for casting the predominant portion of his
dramatic works in verse have already been discussed: we
have seen how he began by using a heightened form of
demotic speech in *Sweeney Agonistes*, using repetition, rhythm,
a chorus and other devices to create a viable stage language.
Stylisation and selectivity contribute to fashion a diction
which although composed of common speech patterns is far
more effective than naturalistic prose for creating the
atmosphere of monotony, erotic fantasy and violence that
Eliot wants. With the commissioning of *The Rock* and *Murder
in the Cathedral* he changed his idiom, but still assembled a
stage medium by extracting from material of religious
provenance those elements most suited to his purpose.

  Eliot himself describes the staple linguistic forms of his
plays in his lecture on 'Poetry and Drama' already referred
to; in the case of *Murder in the Cathedral* he wrote that

> the vocabulary and style could not be exactly those of modern
> conversation . . . because I had to take my audience back to an
> historical event; and they could not afford to be archaic, first
> because archaism would only have suggested the wrong period,
> and second because I wanted to bring home to the audience the
> contemporary relevance of the situation. The style therefore had
> to be *neutral*, committed neither to the present nor to the past. As
> for the versification, I was only aware at this stage that the
> essential was to avoid any echo of Shakespeare. . . . The rhythm
> of regular blank verse had become too remote from the movement
> of modern speech. Therefore what I kept in mind was the
> versification of *Everyman*, hoping that anything unusual in the
> sound of it would be, on the whole, advantageous. An avoidance
> of too much iambic, some use of alliteration, and occasional
> unexpected rhyme, helped to distinguish the versification from
> that of the nineteenth century.
>
>   (*On Poetry and Poets*, p. 80)

This tells us a good deal about the play's language and the

nature of its poetry, but it also omits a good deal too. We have already seen that the influence of Christian phraseology and liturgical forms has a considerable part in giving *Murder in the Cathedral* its characteristic tone. Eliot combines biblical images and tags with his own style of religious writing, much more precise and austere than that of the scriptures, creating a curiously cathedral interior-like texture where drab blank walls are pierced at intervals with moulded monuments or brightly coloured stained-glass windows. In addition there is the idiom in which Eliot successfully conjures up the flavour of medieval life and the close relationship between humankind and the seasonal round, without in either instance having to resort to a spurious 'Merrie England' for his images:

> Fluting in the meadows, viols in the hall,
> Laughter and apple-blossom floating on the water,
> Singing at nightfall, whispering in chambers,
> Fires devouring the winter season. . . .   [p. 246–7]

The text is also rich in animal imagery, some of it highly graphic:

> I have lain on the floor of the sea and breathed with the
> breathing of the sea-anemone, swallowed with ingurgitation of
> the sponge. I have lain in the soil and criticised the worm. In
> the air
> Flirted with the passage of the kite, I have plunged with the kite
> and cowered with the wren. I have felt
> The horn of the beetle, the scale of the viper, the mobile hard
> insensitive skin of the elephant, the evasive flank of the fish.
>   [p. 270]

By contrast, to remind his audience of the 'contemporary relevance of the situation' Eliot will occasionally introduce a passage of blatant anachronism to stress a point, as with the chorus of Tempters while Thomas is at the spiritual crossroads:

QUEEN MARGARET COLLEGE LIBRARY

Man's life is a cheat and a disappointment;
All things are unreal,
Unreal or disappointing:
The Catherine wheel, the pantomime cat,
The prizes given at the children's party,
The prize awarded for the English Essay,
The scholar's degree, the statesman's decoration. [p. 256]

Such mildly satirical speeches render the Knights' addresses
to the spectators a little less of a shock when they occur.

Finally, we should not overlook the sheer variety of tones
and the wealth of verse forms which Eliot deploys, a feature
which distinguishes his verse dramas from those of many
others who followed his example in the '30s and '40s, among
them Ronald Duncan, Norman Nicholson, Anne Ridler and
Christopher Fry. But their work, interesting as it is, lacks the
flexibility of Eliot's command of half a dozen styles and
rhythms. It is hard to get the dactylic metre of the First
Tempter out of one's head, for example:

You see, my Lord, I do not wait upon ceremony:
Here I have come, forgetting all acrimony,
Hoping that your present gravity
Will find excuse for my humble levity . . .   [p. 246]

Equally memorable are the three-line stanzas by the Chorus
which echo the metrics of the *Dies Irae* which is being chanted
off-stage, and the drunken 'jazz' song of the Knights as they
force their way into the Cathedral. And the final Chorus on
which Eliot laboured particularly carefully is a skilful
amalgam of the formal diction of the *Book of Psalms* and of
the *Te Deum* and the contemporary frame of reference that
Eliot insisted upon in all his works of creative literature:

For wherever a saint has dwelt, wherever a martyr has given his
   blood for the blood of Christ,
There is holy ground, and the sanctity shall not depart from it
Though armies trample over it, though sightseers come with
   guide-books looking over it . . .   [p. 281–2]

Few would dispute that the true quality of Eliot's achievement is to be found in the flexibility of his verse movement and the versatility of his command of style, yet there are perhaps reservations about the linguistic texture of *Murder in the Cathedral* which need to be voiced. As poetry its excellence is undeniable, but as dramatic verse it may be criticised occasionally for its opacity, which is at times so dense that the meaning for spectators in the auditorium is irretrievable without recourse to the printed text. Eliot's fondness for ellipsis and aphorism and paradox is one of the pleasures of reading him but in the cut-and-thrust of performance it is somewhat irksome to come up against passages like:

> They know and do not know, what it is to act or suffer.
> They know and do not know, that action is suffering
> And suffering is action. Neither does the agent suffer
> Nor the patient act.   [p. 245]

Or again:

> Not what we call death, but what beyond death is not death.
>   [p. 273]

There is a final point: Eliot himself in 'Poetry and Drama' drew attention to one of the weaknesses of *The Family Reunion* which he felt to be the inclusion of passages of poetry which suspended the dramatic action without furthering the plot or enhancing our knowledge of character. He points out how the mature Shakespeare never introduces a purely poetic line or passage for its own sake but always to support the action or illuminate conduct or mood. *Murder in the Cathedral* is surprisingly free of 'pure poetry', partly because it is a shorter and more intense piece than *The Family Reunion*, but it cannot be denied that there are times when the verse 'covers' a situation rather than illuminating it; such a point is undoubtedly that crucial sequence before Thomas recovers his equilibrium following the Fourth Tempter's insidious revelations. What the dramatic situation requires is some insight into Thomas's mind; what we hear is marvellous verse.

And this perhaps highlights a very deep problem with the play, that the immensely powerful forms of verse never coalesce any more than the variegated groups of characters do; Thomas is perhaps necessarily an isolated and lonely figure, but the fact of his lack of contact with the Women who fear him and form him, the Priests who do not fully comprehend his purposes and the Knights who oppose him, is reflected in the contrasting separations between the verse forms. This may be a significant factor in convincing several critics that *Murder in the Cathedral* is less a play than a verbal opera, or as Bernard Bergonzi says, 'a finely scored oratorio'.

Between this play and *The Cocktail Party* Eliot revised his notions of dramatic verse in creating a mode of versification which could enable him to handle the rhythms of contemporary conversational speech as heard from the lips of modern-day figures rather than from those of the personages of history. He therefore set out to evolve a mode of stage poetry which could slide effortlessly from handling everyday commonplaces to expressing intense states of mind and intimations of values lying outside the range of mundane existence. For this purpose, says the playwright,

> What I worked out is substantially what I have continued to employ: a line of varying length and varying number of syllables, with a caesura [pause] and three stresses. The caesura and the stresses may come at different places, almost anywhere in the line; the stresses may be close together or well separated by light syllables; the only rule being that there must be one stress on one side of the caesura and two on the other.
>
> (*On Poetry and Poets*, p. 82)

The poetry of *The Cocktail Party* therefore is a far less ostensibly striking feature of the work than it is in *Murder in the Cathedral*; indeed, the author himself went so far as to wonder whether 'there is any poetry in the play at all'. To which the reply must be 'It depends what you mean by poetry'. Certainly the 'recitative and aria' aspect of the earlier plays is not present; there is little of the lyrical writing which we can discover even in the relatively chaste idiom of *The Family Reunion*; certainly the excitingly graphic writing of the choruses in *Murder in the Cathedral* is hardly ever given any opportunity for display, so much so that some commentators seized on Reilly's quotation from Shelley in the final act as if it were a spoonful of water in an arid desert, simply because its freedom from the necessity for temperate restraint contrasted with the rather tepid and limp pattern of versification Eliot had imposed on himself in what some saw as the masochism of self-denial.

There is no doubt that in many respects the poetry 'works' in *The Cocktail Party*, given Eliot's aims: it does not draw undue attention to itself, and is thus just as likely to be *heard* by an audience as if it were prose, although on the page it clearly looks like verse. Eliot's flexible line is very easily modulated through conventional banalities like

> Oh, no, Alex, don't bring me any cheese

to 'deadpan' pronouncements like

> A common interest in the moving pictures
> Frequently brings young people together

or witty Wildean aphorisms like

> I am simply in hell. Where there are no doctors –
> At least, not in a professional capacity.

It also works quite well when Reilly is gravely and professionally advising his 'clients' for their own spiritual benefit and using his authority to analyse their paths to their own forms of salvation:

> I can reconcile you to the human condition,
> The condition to which some who have gone as far as you
> Have succeeded in returning. They may remember
> The vision they have had, but they cease to regret it,
> Maintain themselves by the common routine,
> Learn to avoid excessive expectation . . .   [p. 417]

This sort of verse copes quite happily when the aim is
humour or light conversation or even earnest instruction, but
it is less successful when the situation calls for passion or any
kind of intense emotional feeling, as several of Celia's speeches
in Act Two seem to demonstrate. Her ability to articulate
her own sensations of guilt and isolation seems less implausible
than the drab and clinical idiom the poet employs to convey
them:

> I have thought at moments that the ecstasy is real
> Although those who experience it may have no reality.
> For what happened is remembered like a dream
> In which one is exalted by the intensity of loving
> In the spirit, a vibration of delight
> Without desire, for desire is fulfilled
> In the delight of loving.   [p. 417]

Even if one can come at the meaning – quite a sophisticated
one – and accept the validity of the statement – quite an
unfashionable one – one longs for a little colour, a telling
image, to personalise and humanise the self-effacing austerity
of the poetry.

Thus, despite Eliot's hope of forging an idiom for drama in
which 'the border of those feelings which only music can
express' might be touched without losing contact with the
'ordinary everyday world', his dramatic verse at these
moments seems to prove just as flat and restricting as
speeches in the medium of naturalistic prose which Eliot the
critic so despaired of. There is a failure to 'sing and shine'
quite as damaging as anything Yeats found in Ibsen. Dry,
pedantic, fussy, too concerned with 'If and Perhaps and
But' – these are some of the charges levelled against Eliot's
dramatic verse; as John Bayley wrote in the *Review* for
November 1962:

> ... like the rhythm of *Hiawatha*, it is not only comical and fatally
> insistent, but it also determines, as all such rhythms must, the
> actual nature of what *is* being said. One knows somehow what
> an Eliot character is going to say as soon as he begins speaking.
> ... Though theoretically flexible, the rhythm is really dominating

to the point where it becomes impossible for any character to *surprise* us, or to strike a personal or idiosyncratic note. . . .

(p. 7)

It seems a pity that Eliot who could in his poems produce images so highly charged with resonance and emotion, and so create a personal idiom so authoritative and individual, should in his plays have deliberately chosen to fabricate a poetry so lacking in personality and linguistic charge. Of course, it might well be argued that there was scarcely a writer in Britain in Eliot's day who could have made as intelligent and spirited an attempt at devising a form of stage poetry which would have coped with the dual requirements of daily life and 'the mystery that invests being'. It represents, however, a kind of poetic minimalism which issuing as it does from one of the most exciting poets of the twentieth century cannot fail in many respects to disappoint.

PART TWO: PERFORMANCE

7 INTRODUCTION

In this section the following productions have been selected
for close attention:
Murder in the Cathedral staged in the chapter house of
Canterbury Cathedral by the Cathedral Players, 15 June
1935 (Becket: Robert Speaight; Director: E. Martin Browne),
subsequently transferring to the Mercury and the Duchess
Theatres, London; at the Old Vic Theatre, London, by the
Old Vic Company, 31 March 1953 (Becket: Robert Donat;
Director: Robert Helpmann); at the Aldwych Theatre,
London, by the Royal Shakespeare Company, 31 August
1972 (Becket: Richard Pasco; Director: Terry Hands).
The Cocktail Party staged at the Lyceum Theatre, Edinburgh,
22 August 1949 (Reilly: Alec Guinness; Celia: Irene Worth;
Director: E. Martin Browne), subsequently transferring to
the Henry Miller Theatre, New York; at the New Theatre,
London, 3 May 1950 (Reilly: Rex Harrison; Celia: Margaret
Leighton; Director: E. Martin Browne); at the Chichester
Festival Theatre, 28 May 1968 (Reilly: Sir Alec Guinness;
Celia: Eileen Atkins; Director: Guinness), subsequently
transferring to Wyndham's and the Haymarket Theatres,
London).
The genesis of *Murder in the Cathedral* is exceptionally well
documented and, as a result, has been recounted many times.
Basically, it came into being as a response to a crusade led
by a group of Anglican clerics and laymen to revive religious
drama as an instrument of instruction and inspiration in the
late 1920s and early 1930s. Its leading spirit was George
Bell, Dean of Canterbury from 1924 to 1928, who during his
short period of office revolutionised life in and around the
great building of which he had custody. His enthusiasm for

literature and drama blossomed into a commission in the
summer of 1927 for John Masefield (created Poet Laureate in
1930) to write an original nativity play for presentation in
the nave of the cathedral; Gustav Holst undertook the music,
Charles Ricketts the costume designs and Masefield himself
directed, the cast being anonymous as far as the audience
was concerned. Its success led to the establishment of an
annual Canterbury Festival of Music and Drama, with a
dramatic presentation at the heart of the celebrations: the
first took place in August 1929, when the celebrated
Maddermarket Company from Norwich under Nugent Monck
presented *Everyman* at the cathedral's West Door, and
Marlowe's *Dr Faustus* in the chapter house, the change of
venue being dictated, not by any impiety in the presentation
of Masefield's *The Coming of Christ* the previous year, but to
the almost insuperable problems of the cathedral's acoustics.
Not that the chapter house was in any sense a particularly
viable alternative as a place to produce plays in: its own
acoustics were notorious thanks to a high wooden ceiling; all
exits and entrances in the early years had to be made through
a solitary door down a long central aisle; lighting could only
be of the simplest kind; the curtainless stage itself was of
extraordinarily idiosyncratic dimensions. As E. Martin
Browne was to write:

> The Chapter House, despite the historic series of productions it
> housed, is a building for which I have no affection. Its reverberent
> acoustic makes speaking a misery, and its platform stage was
> thirty-six feet wide by only nine feet deep. At the stage front, a
> flight of steps led down to the centre aisle, ninety feet long, which
> was the only way in or out of the building. Stage lighting is
> rendered almost useless by the huge windows. (*Two in One*, p. 93)

However, in spite of the drawbacks a sequence of
productions was mounted here during the ensuing Festivals,
though it seems clear that the standard was not always of the
highest, Tennyson's *Becket* presented in 1932 being staged
with more enthusiasm than polish. However, Laurence
Irving, grandson of the great Victorian star and an early
associate of Bell's, took over the stage design in 1933 and

1934, building as an aid to projection a permanent open stage and utilising screens to provide a more flexible *mise-en-scène*, including primitive wings. This proved effective in the presentation of a revamped *Becket* in 1933 and of *The Young King*, Laurence Binyon's sequel to the events described in Tennyson's play, which made use of the same mode of staging, in 1934. In the light of Eliot's careful avoidance of 'too much iambic' in *Murder in the Cathedral*, it is noteworthy that Binyon's piece employs a pseudo-Shakespearean idiom which can hardly be reckoned effective or easy to deliver.

By this time Bell's dynamism and progressive ideas had taken him away from Canterbury to the bishopric of nearby Chichester, from whence he could still maintain a keen interest in the fortunes of the Canterbury Festival. One of his most unusual actions after taking up office had been to appoint a Diocesan Director of Drama, an unprecedented step which indicated a continuing belief in the potential contained in religious drama. The appointee was an Oxford graduate of 30, whose main activity since 1926 had been as a lecturer in speech and drama in America, where he had added to the theatre experience he had obtained through university dramatics. E. Martin Browne was also an ardent Anglo-Catholic, and his new post offered him the opportunity of combining his twin enthusiasms. He and Bell agreed that if drama was to play a part in the religious life of the diocese, then it should be worthily and competently mounted and performed, and for several years Browne and his highly supportive wife, Henzie Raeburn, organised and supervised plays and readings throughout the Chichester area. It was Bell who introduced the Brownes to Eliot in the winter of 1930, and it was Browne who persuaded the Director of the London Diocesan Churches Fund to commission the script of *The Rock* from Eliot in September 1933.

It appears as if Bell was not entirely satisfied with the Canterbury Festival plays after the specially commissioned *Coming of Christ* had gone its way; revivals of medieval and Renaissance classics, restagings of Victorian romantic chronicles, remodellings of Georgian blank-verse imitations, were unlikely to kindle the hearts and minds of the postwar generation, and Bell hankered, it would seem, after something a little more obviously 'contemporary'. With the success of *The Rock*, there seemed little doubt as to who should have the privilege of receiving the request for the next specially commissioned work for Canterbury, and using monies accruing from *The Coming of Christ*, Bell and Laurence Irving invited Eliot, not long after *The Rock* had completed its run at Sadler's Wells, to write a play for the 1935 Festival. Eliot's only stipulation appears to have been that E. Martin Browne, with whom he had established a very happy and comfortable relationship during the production of *The Rock*, should direct at Canterbury.

The development of the play from first drafts to final version has been exhaustively dealt with in Browne's *The Making of T. S. Eliot's Plays*, the story of its production in his joint autobiographical venture with his wife, *Two in One*, and in Kenneth Pickering's thorough study of the whole Canterbury enterprise, *Drama in the Cathedral*. The nature of Browne's collaboration with the author on the texts will be considered in a later chapter, but the broad outline of the background to the first performances may be sketched in here. Eliot visited Canterbury and decided at once that Becket must once again be the focal point for yet another Canterbury offering, thus disconcerting Laurence Irving, his host, who admitted in an interview tape-recorded in 1975 that '*We* thought we'd had enough of Thomas a Becket – but of course he was quite right – it was *entirely new*.'

The title originally suggested was *Fear in the Way*, a reference from the passage in *Ecclesiastes* XII alluded to by the Third Priest, and it was Henzie Raeburn who put to Eliot the possibility that a title analogous to that of a crime novel of the Agatha Christie type might be more attractive and less portentous. (Eliot was a Sherlock Holmes fan, and indeed the staccato questions and answers exchanged between the Second Tempter and Becket quoted on an earlier page are indebted to 'the Musgrave Ritual' from *The Memoirs*.)

The cast was chiefly composed of those stalwart amateur players who had sustained the earlier Festival productions; the only professionals were Browne's friend and Oxford contemporary, Robert˙ Speaight; Frank Napier who had recently at the Old Vic played York to Maurice Evans's Richard II; and Browne himself. The important Chorus on which so much depends were not recruited locally, but were students from the Central School of Dramatic Art, coached in London by the redoubtable Elsie Fogarty, a leading pioneer of the techniques of choral speaking, who had trained the speakers in *The Rock*. Eleven volunteers were found, but because of academic commitments they could only attend two rehearsals *in situ*, the first of which was spent attempting to compensate for the atrocious resonance, which was partially negated by discovering the direction in which voices might be safely projected without distorting the sound. The complete cast was only assembled for the single dress rehearsal.

The original run was for only eight performances, and while the more discriminating playgoers, critics and Festival patrons were impressed, it is significant that only one London manager felt it worth his while to travel to Canterbury and see for himself what was going on. This was Ashley Dukes, the cultured and well-to-do owner of the minute Mercury Theatre, a converted church property in Notting Hill Gate, which could seat 136 and offered a stage only 2 feet deeper than that at Canterbury, but with a projecting apron platform to give additional depth. He asked Browne to stage the play there, with an all-professional cast, and this was done on 1 November 1935, the only amateurs being the students playing the Chorus, although this involved frequent changes of personnel, all handled now by Elsie Fogarty's deputy, Gwynneth Thorburn. An amazingly successful run then ensued, and when Dukes took the piece off on 16 May 1936, it went on tour to Oxford, Cambridge and Dublin, to return to the Mercury in September. On 30 October it transferred to the Duchess Theatre, a far larger auditorium holding 491 and situated just off the Strand; here it enjoyed another run of 5 months. Further interest was added by a BBC television transmission of the play on 21 December. In 1937 it went on two lengthy tours in the provinces, being staged at Leeds, Manchester and Edinburgh; in June the company returned to London to present a five-week run of the play at the Old Vic, and this was succeeded by a week of presentations at the Tewkesbury Festival, with the west front of the Norman abbey there as backdrop. In the early part of 1938 Browne and Ashley Dukes transported the production to the States, where it had brief runs in Boston and New York. During the war years it was toured by the Pilgrim Players, headed by the Brownes, to a wide variety of unlikely locations, audiences travelling miles in the blackout to see Browne himself as Becket, and when Ashley Dukes on the cessation of hostilities offered him the Mercury Theatre to present a season of 'New Plays by Poets', Eliot's best-known play was inserted into the repertoire, where it enjoyed a three-month run from February 1948, after being staged at the Edinburgh Festival of 1947 at the Gateway Theatre, along with *The Family Reunion*. In 1951 a film version appeared and two years later the first professional revival in London was essayed by Robert Helpmann at the Old Vic, with Robert Donat (whom ill-health would shortly force to retire) playing his last role as Becket. In 1972 Terry Hands's production for the Royal Shakespeare Company proved that interest in Eliot's drama, commissioned though it might have been for a specific occasion, had by no means waned, and it was the 'runaway success of the season'.

The history of *The Cocktail Party* is nothing like as lengthy or as glamorous, appearing to have its origins in Martin Browne's invitation following the 1947 Edinburgh Festival productions that Eliot should compose a piece for the following year's celebrations. The playwright made a start early in 1948, having a first draft entitled *One-Eyed Reilly* ready for discussion with the director by June, but it was clear that the finished work would not be ready in time for the 1948 Festival. By January 1949 the piece was nearing completion, and it was Browne's hope that the newly appointed director at the Old Vic, Hugh Hunt, would agree that it might receive its first Edinburgh production by that Company, but Hunt did not wish to commit himself to Browne as the play's producer, and felt that the bare synopsis provided was not enough from which to visualise a potential cast for the production. Eliot refused to consent to entrust his new work to any other director than Browne, on grounds of both loyalty and self-interest, and the matter was resolved by the discovery of an impressario, Henry Sherek, willing to back the production for the Edinburgh Festival that summer. Sherek was an unlikely sponsor for a play in verse written by a thinking man and a Nobel Prize winner, but as a man of the theatre with an immense knowledge of its technicalities, he proved invaluable to both Eliot and his director whose theatre experience had been gained in its more esoteric corners.

The Cocktail Party, which opened on 22 August 1949 at the Lyceum Theatre, was one of the great successes of the Festival, and attracted an immense amount of attention during its run of a single week, Alec Guinness's film commitments precluding a longer sequence. A move straight into a West End playhouse would have been the ideal sequel, but this proved difficult to arrange, and the play was seen next on Broadway, at the Henry Miller Theatre from 21 January 1950, with most of the original cast, excluding Ursula Jeans who created Lavinia and Donald Houston who had played Peter. Here again *The Cocktail Party* achieved a considerable success, with a glittering first night ensuring that attendance of at least one performance became *de rigueur* among New York socialites. The play was widely argued over, praised to the skies, denigrated, and so became the piece that everyone had to see in order to find out what all the fuss was about. The New York run eventually extended to over 200 performances and its popularity on Broadway enabled Sherek to secure the New Theatre in London for its première in the English capital. It had been hoped to delay the opening until June when the New York cast would be available, but it had to be brought forward to early May, so a completely new production had to be mounted with a fresh cast. Rex Harrison (better known even in 1950 as a film actor, though the cardigan of Professor Higgins had not yet become permanently draped round his shoulders) played Reilly; Celia was Margaret Leighton and Ian Hunter undertook Edward; Donald Houston returned to the cast as

Peter. The London production opened on 3 June, and in August three members of the New York team replaced their London counterparts; although Harrison had to quit the company in August, the run did not conclude until February 1951. The vogue for *The Cocktail Party* led to a sprightly parody of Eliot's various styles in the *New Statesman*, in which the commercial triumph of 'this metaphysical mime' was not allowed to pass without sardonic comment:

> This is the vulgarest success, blasting
> A hitherto immaculate reputation . . .

In May 1968 the play was successfully revived to general critical approval at the Festival Theatre in Chichester, with Guinness recreating his role as Reilly and directing; his was reckoned to be the definitive version of the part, despite the lapse of almost twenty years since his first venture, and Eileen Atkins as Celia won the highest praise. The production transferred to London on 6 November 1968, Richard Leech replacing Hubert Gregg as Alex and Mark Kingston taking over from David Collings as Peter.

8   THE AUTHOR'S ROLE

No one who had ever seen T. S. Eliot in his literary infancy would have supposed him born to be a playwright. Yet he found himself from his mid-40s onwards drawn into a series of theatrical ventures for which he provided a set of highly original, experimental and provocative scripts. Therefore it would seem important to establish, in the case of *Murder in the Cathedral* and *The Cocktail Party*, the kind of influence which their original conditions of performance had on the texts of the plays as they have come down to us.

In some respects Eliot's lack of contact with the commercial theatre of the interwar years was not necessarily a bad thing,

1. Canterbury Cathedral Chapter House, site of the first performances of *Murder in the Cathedral*. Photograph © Pitkin Pictorials

2. Becket (Robert Speaight) and the Tempters from the 1935 production of *Murder in the Cathedral*. Photograph by J.W. Debenham, courtesy of the Victoria and Albert Museum

3. The finale of *Murder in the Cathedral* as staged at the Mercury Theatre, 1935, with Becket and members of the Chorus. Photograph as above

4. Robert Donat as Becket with the Tempters, Priests and Chorus from the Old Vic production of *Murder in the Cathedral* in 1953. Photograph by Houston Rogers, courtesy of the Victoria and Albert Museum

5. The Murder of Becket from the 1953 Old Vic production of *Murder in the Cathedral*. Photograph as above

6. Act III of *The Cocktail Party* as staged at the New Theatre, in 1950, with Rex Harrison as Harcourt-Reilly. Photograph by Anthony Buckley, courtesy of the Victoria and Albert Museum

7. The 'libation scene' from the Chichester Festival Theatre production of *The Cocktail Party* in 1968, with Alec Guinness as Harcourt-Reilly. Photograph © John Timbers

for as Martin Browne wrote in 'The Poet and the Stage' published in *The Penguin New Writing* 31 (1947):

> what the theatre needs from [the poet] is a redemption from naturalism, which no one too deeply soaked in the craft of the present-day theatre could effect. His freedom may enable him to evolve more easily the methods that suit his purposes.   (p. 82)

But Browne goes on to note that there is a counterbalancing drawback:

> lack of contact with the theatre has imposed an ignorance more fundamental: he has no experience of the actor's art except from 'the front', and no means of discovering what are the true reasons for the success or failure of a line or a situation . . . So when he labours to create his own play, he has to judge his work, not by the actor's effort to bring it to life in rehearsal, but by his own ear as he hears it in his head, and his own eye scanning the page.   (p. 82–3)

One can more readily understand then why Eliot clung to a sympathetic director for the first presentations of all his plays after *Sweeney*, and much of Browne's book, *The Making of T. S. Eliot's Plays* (1969), is devoted to a painstakingly detailed account of the changes mutually hammered out in order to make Eliot's work fit the requirements of the stage. This material can be considered and assessed at leisure: what follows is a bald outline of the principal revisions and alterations called for.

In the case of *Murder in the Cathedral* much was dictated by the nature of the chapter house setting which Eliot viewed in December 1934, before getting down to the business of composition. But Browne makes it clear that Eliot already had in mind a play with a Chorus and that it may have been Rupert Doone, director of the Group Theatre, who persuaded him to use verse for almost the whole of the piece. It was also Doone who suggested that the visitors from Becket's past, required to bridge the gap between Thomas's arrival in Canterbury and the events leading to his murder, should be treated as images from the Archbishop's mind, rather than as flesh-and-blood visitants as Browne had suggested. Despite some bafflement for those whose historical knowledge was a little deficient, the Tempters help Thomas to resolve his own doubts in time to preach his confident Christmas sermon, as well as providing an audience with the contextual data it requires to understand something of the feud between Church and State. It was Browne who suggested doubling the parts of the Tempters in the first production with those of the Knights not only in order to facilitate understanding that the enemies without and the enemies within Becket's mind are related, but because Browne was reluctant to dilute the quality of his mainly amateur cast by recruiting too many local actors! But even when an all-professional cast was engaged for the Mercury opening, the device was retained. Eliot eventually came to demur at the notion, and in the Old Vic production of 1953 the parts were not doubled, although doubling was restored at the Aldwych in 1972. Future directors are presumably free to choose.

Performance conditions also had a bearing on the script in other ways: Eliot's papers suggest that he was very conscious of the time factor imposed on him, that his play should only run for 90 minutes without an interval, perhaps a condition governed by the organisers' awareness that the audience would be seated on rush-seated chairs in a setting not highly conducive to the enjoyment of drama. Because of this limitation means had to be devised to suggest the passage of time, other than via the programme: it was Browne who suggested the scene at the beginning of what is now Part II where the Priests enter with banners signifying the three Feast Days which follow Christmas, each of which has relevance to the martyrdom about to take place. Eliot added the touch whereby the Priests celebrate, in advance as it were of the martyrdom, Becket's enrolment in the Church's calendar of the saints.

The actual physical aspects of the chapter house and their effect on staging the play are more the concern of the next chapter; all one may say here is that Eliot's script shows an awareness of the restrictions dictated by the shallow wide platform and the single entrance down the 90-feet long aisle.

Indeed, the entries through the auditorium are made a feature of the action: the processional arrivals of the Priests in Part II, the twin eruptions of the Knights and, above all, the final retreat with Becket's body borne out through the audience into the cloisters with the Priests and Chorus carrying candles while a litany was sung, all helped to make the most of the setting. Certainly, nothing like this was possible at the minute Mercury, and of course the historical bonus – that the actor's body was being carried through the very cloisters down which the real assassins had escaped in 1170 – was unique to Canterbury.

The Cocktail Party, once again, offers far tamer data, in that its production was always planned for a conventional proscenium-style auditorium, and exigencies of time and space were not a crucial factor. In *Murder in the Cathedral* Eliot was creating his own prototype of a religious drama; in his subsequent works he was engaged in large measure in making replicas of a dramatic genre which already existed, even if he hoped to secrete a doctrinal time bomb somewhere in its fabric. None the less, Browne's book contains some interesting indications of the sorts of revisions the early drafts underwent to create a piece which satisfied the more theatrical demands. The play as originally conceived contained too little action; it was much too static, consisting for much of its length in a series of duologues, something which does not mar the more hieratic *Murder*, but which produces monotony on the illusionistic stage. Browne suggested breaking up the sequence of interviews by employing Alex and Julia to interrupt at intervals in the latter part of i i, i ii and Act ii. The device of the telegrams was interpolated in i iii for much the same reasons. This also permitted a necessary development in the characters of Alex and Julia, so that their dual function in the action came as less of a shock.

Browne was also able to advise Eliot to create fewer scenic divisions in the play, a far stricter necessity in a proscenium-type playhouse where the 'curtains' have to be reduced to a minimum. It also seems to have been agreed to make the tone of the earlier drafts lighter, with comedy more emphasised and more small domestic touches of detail helping both to create verisimilitude and disperse portentousness. Even the introduction of the Caterer's Man was made for this purpose. Perhaps for the same reason, Reilly's quotation from Shelley was removed during the New York run, though restored for the London production.

Some problems were never entirely eradicated; Browne argued early on that the 'libation scene' was too unlike anything else in the play, and it may still be felt to be so, although much depends on the style in which it is played. The performers have to be careful not to lose sight of their more mundane selves in handling it. There is also the issue of Celia's reported death, not so much its horrific nature, which was toned down after the Edinburgh performances on the grounds of gratuitous detail, but because it was felt to result in an ensuing anti-climax, in that no clear dramatic action emerged from its revelation. Adjustments were made to show that Peter, Edward and Lavinia resume their lives in an increased understanding of why Celia died, but there seems to be no way in which Celia's experience can be fully assimilated into the ultimate moments of the action. Yet the average audience is perhaps more interested in the way in which Edward and Lavinia have recemented their marriage than in the casting problems of film makers or the hazards of missionary work in an unheard-of island in the East.

9 THE DIRECTORS' ROLE

It must be abundantly clear by now that E. Martin Browne (1900–1980) is a figure of considerable importance in any account of T. S. Eliot's work in the theatre. Not only did he direct all the original productions of the plays after the fragmentary *Sweeney*, but played a central role in assisting Eliot to achieve the effects he wanted in the dramatic medium. The poet gained in him a staunch ally and friend, and Browne found in Eliot a writer, the realisation of whose work on stage enabled him to combine his own passions for poetry, drama and the Christian religion.

Browne's background was undeniably upper-class; educated at Eton and Christ Church, Oxford, he was an ardent Anglo-Catholic, like Eliot and like many of those of his generation and stock who were not wooed away from religion by the newer agnostic doctrines of the postwar years. To the outsider there is something a little cosy and élitist about such relatively affluent and secure figures in whom High Church tastes and theatrical enterprise went hand-in-hand, though it is easy to see how a belief in ritual and ceremonial provided a common denominator. But in reading accounts of the lives of those members of society in whom Christianity and privilege complemented each other, one cannot help being forcibly reminded of Lady Bracknell's words:

> Every luxury that money could buy, including christening, had been lavished on you by your fond and doting parents.

More seriously, this sense of election to an exclusive club of believers with its somewhat esoteric air and its danger of tending towards mutual admiration could lead to a fatal parochialism in artistic matters; Browne's integrity and abilities as a director prevented this from vitiating the case of Eliot, though there are some who feel that Becket's seeming 'lack of charity' and his failure to make meaningful contact with the Women of Canterbury is symptomatic of the exclusiveness they detect in his creators. In the same way, the sneaking notion that salvation is one further right reserved for the well-to-do professional classes sometimes comes to the forefront of one's mind when perusing *The Cocktail Party*.

However, Browne's staging initiatives, particularly in the case of *Murder in the Cathedral*, are vitally important to this study; he availed himself of both local and imported talent to combat the snags of playing in the chapter house, and to bring out the full effectiveness of Eliot's achievement. He utilised Laurence Irving's permanent setting as devised for the 1933 *Becket* and *The Young King* in 1934, which consisted of a number of Gordon Craig-style screens seven feet high

which matched the fourteenth-century arcading round the
walls and were painted to blend with them. These could
provide the scenery behind which players could be concealed
prior to the play's commencement, and also serve as wings
into which they could 'exit'. Browne added a double flight of
steps by which the performers entering down the lengthy
aisle could reach the stage, and for the Chorus he had
erected two platforms at either side of the main playing area,
where they were compelled to remain through much of the
action, the stage offering no means of departure for eleven
women. This helped to reduce the pressure on space on the
main platform, but in a scene like the one in which Becket
wrestles with his conscience, it was impossible to introduce
much movement. The Tempters who had entered up the
aisle retired to positions in the backstage arcading and
advanced on Becket for the 'trio' between Priests, Chorus
and themselves. Then as Becket regained poise, they beat a
retreat through the auditorium, to change into costumes as
Knights, which the continuous nature of the action meant
they did during Becket's sermon.

Costumes were of course centrally important in a production
which was competing with a medieval chapter house for its
impact. Colour was needed to divert the eye from the
surroundings, and Browne turned to Stella Mary Pearce
(later Newton) who had handled the designs for *The Rock*, to
devise outfits that would catch the play's spirit while not
being slavishly in period. The Chorus in pale green headcloths
were given robes in two shades of green, divided by bold
horizontal patterns of red and blue, supplying the effect of
early stained glass, and though Ashley Dukes wrote of 'visible
signs of the art-and-craft spirit', they were genuinely effective.
The Priests and Becket were more conventionally clad, the
temptation of putting the saint in full vestments for the
sermon being resisted. The most enterprising designs were
featured in the Tempters' costumes: the predominating colour
was bright yellow, and each was given an element in his
clothing to clarify both his temperament and the nature of
the temptation represented: the First's coronet incorporated
a suggestion of the 'topper' of a pleasure-seeking 'city gent';

the Second bore a suggestion of modern medals; the Third wore heraldic checks which gave the impression of plus fours, to which his stick shaped a little like a golf club gave support; the Fourth, dressed to resemble Becket as befitted his other self, had crowns and palms imprinted on his costume suggesting the tangible rewards of martyrdom. (At the Mercury the Tempters wore darker rigouts.) The Priests' banners which are almost the only vital properties in the piece (and even these arc not essential) added to the iconographical effect, stressed at the murder by having it slowly mimed to mirror Canterbury's famous medieval painting of the outrage. The needful liturgical music was performed by the warden and students of a local theological college, singing from a specially erected gallery above the entrance at the rear of the chapter house.

It is of interest to compare this original staging with the visual treatment the play received in the production by Helpmann at the Old Vic in 1953 and that of Terry Hands for the Royal Shakespeare Company in 1972. Neither at the Old Vic nor the Aldwych could there be the ecclesiastical and local associations which had enabled the first presentations to make a significant part of their impact, regardless of their direction. The Old Vic producer strove therefore to create the atmosphere of a medieval place of worship, relying on raised levels, steps, fabricated stonework, heavy fluted columns and 'the plainness of oak and stone'. For Terry Hands Abdul Farrah preferred suggestion to solidity, creating space with rough hessian and silver foil, raking his stage and 'paving' it with flagstones, one of which obligingly rose on a stalk to form Becket's pulpit. A featureless altar made a useful focal point in Part II and the Knights danced round it in exultant mood, but the withered tree of Part I was more evocative of Beckett, Samuel than Becket, Thomas. It also seemed distracting and gratuitous to finish by erecting a hefty cross of wood and canvas on stage for no other reason than to form the final tableau at its foot. It was nothing like as effective in use as the splendid Romanesque banners for the three holy days, on which the women worked as they spoke the initial chorus of Part II.

Costumes in the Old Vic production were unremarkable in their generic medievalism; this was not a period of great experimentation in the English theatre, least of all at the Old Vic which tended at this juncture to mount simple, orthodox versions of the classical repertoire. The Chorus here wore plain headcloths and plain unpatterned dresses. The accent in the 1972 rendering was on making the costumes look rough and well-worn, following the Brechtian convention as pioneered by the Berliner Ensemble. Becket took off the black cloak he wore initially to reveal a tattered hairshirt, and all the robes were of coarse material, though the First Tempter wore a shiny substance as his role dictated. Charles Lewsen in *The Times* for 1 September 1972 objected most strongly to the way the Chorus was garbed:

> 'The scrubbers and sweepers of Canterbury' . . . are dressed in the kind of all purpose pauper's weeds, carefully torn and assiduously stained, which I thought *Mother Courage* had put an end to. This generalised show of poverty places them in a social limbo – acceptable enough in an old-fashioned way when they are agonizing in unison; but when the lines are broken up to encourage realistic delivery . . . this is made unbelievable by the clothes and by the women's lack of employment . . . .

Martin Esslin too in *Plays and Players* felt that peasant dress and middle-class accents were at odds with each other; the point will need to be taken up in the next chapter.

Perhaps the most daring dramatic stroke at the Aldwych – and yet it seemed in keeping with Eliot's intention – was the handling of the speeches of justification by the Knights; these were delivered with the four men, dressed in black collarless jackets, sitting at a table speaking into microphones, which certainly assisted the analogy drawn with contemporary techniques of political debate.

The Cocktail Party obviously offers fewer opportunities for major initiatives in staging; if the aim is to make the play's surface resemble that of a smart up-to-date entertainment set in elegant surroundings, one cannot stray far from that ambience, though one suspects that a present-day production would be less concerned to give the play all the detailed paraphernalia and verisimilitude that featured in all three presentations under scrutiny here. Something stylised and suggestive – without concern for each mantelpiece ornament and drinks tray – might help *The Cocktail Party* to establish at once that its concerns were not solely with material matters. As it is, even the set for the Guinness production of 1968 – post-Beckett and Pinter as it was – still went for realism, the large oil-painting of the 1950 version being replaced by an enormous tiger-skin rug, as if to prove that Julia in Act One had been right and there were tigers after all. Costumes in every version could never be anything other than conventional for the period in which the play is set, that is, 'today'. However, it is notable that a degree of visual symbolism was detectable in the Chichester production, which almost certainly owed something to the advent of the 'Comedy of Menace'; in the 'libation scene' in Act Two, Julia and Alex donned dark glasses, which complementing Reilly's monocle, gave them a very sinister, 'other-worldly' effect, and assisted the impression that here were creatures from another spiritual realm. Not that the first production was unalive to a little judicious 'naturalistic symbolism' as the *Glasgow Herald* for 31 August 1949 makes clear:

> To reduce Mr Eliot's play to a fashion parade would be unseemly; nevertheless this cocktail party was dressed in the newest styles ... and definitely reflected the coming trends. Moreover, one part depended on a change in type of dress to convey to the audience its first inkling that there was something unusual here. This fell to the lot of Miss Cathleen Nesbitt [as Julia] who, wearing a floral-patterned, fluttering dress and fussy hat, is first of all the dithering guest who provides the light relief; when she appears in a later scene quietly dressed in a plain black frock, we have our first hint that she has a dual role in the scheme of things.

10   The Players' Roles

Since such a wide range of performers was involved in the several productions of *Murder in the Cathedral* and *The Cocktail Party* under review, in this chapter it has been necessary to focus on a handful of players, and priority has been given to the three Beckets and to the handling of the Chorus. In the case of *The Cocktail Party* attention has been concentrated on the contrasting Reillys of Alec Guinness and Rex Harrison, and on the Celias of Irene Worth, Margaret Leighton and Eileen Atkins.

Pride of place must undoubtedly go to Robert Speaight who created the part of Becket at Canterbury. Speaight like Martin Browne came from a well-to-do background, went to the famous English public school of Haileybury and on to Lincoln College, Oxford, where he became secretary of the University Dramatic Society and appeared as Peer Gynt and Falstaff. He went into the Liverpool Repertory Company, appeared in a number of London productions and at the Old Vic played a range of Shakespearean roles including Edmund in *Lear*, King John, Fluellen, Cassius, Malvolio and Hamlet. At the time he was invited to play Becket in 1935 he was 31 against the saint's 56, and 5'8½" in height to Becket's staggering 6'4". However, Browne, who knew him from Oxford days, felt that as a devout Roman Catholic convert, an admirer of Eliot, and as one of the finest speakers of verse on the English stage, Speaight could scarcely be bettered. The actor was also no mean writer, and has since been able to articulate for posterity much of what he felt about performing the part.

Speaight has recorded how on his first sight of the script, he felt that Becket was thin on theatrical opportunities, a passive protagonist who lacked initiative. But he came to see that 'the initiatives were the initiatives of grace, and Becket's business was obedience'. A less committed Christian than Speaight might not have picked this up, of course, and indeed his entire Canterbury performance does appear to one who was not there (though born not 30 miles away later that summer) to have carried the hallmark of great personal conviction, and to have been as much an act of worship as a dramatic impersonation. Yet it is only right to state that Speaight did not find Becket a completely sympathetic figure: he believed there to be a self-dramatising element in his personality, and while impersonating him on over a thousand occasions, 'never felt near to him as a man'. He also wished that the author had offered a little more for an actor to build on:

> there was the problem of giving concrete shape to a character which had been conceived, designedly, in the abstract. These bones were beautiful, but they needed the integument of flesh. I had to snatch at any clue which would suggest the man that Becket once had been, as well as the man he had become.
>
> ('With Becket . . .', in Allen Tate (ed.) *T. S. Eliot*, 1966, Penguin edn, 1971, p. 188)

This is perhaps the reason why Speaight discovered the impersonal device of the sermon to be the *pièce de résistance* of the whole play for him, and had to fight against the temptation to linger it out. It is interesting that Martin Browne records Speaight's preference for remaining seated during the four temptations, not meeting the eyes of his interrogators except for those of the hypnotic Fourth Tempter played by Browne himself. Was his immobility devised to stress Becket's passivity, his obedience or the somewhat limited playing space available? Or was it to avoid drawing undue attention to the player's medium height? (At least one photograph shows him posed on a step to address the Women!)

Opinions on the quality of Speaight's performance are not easy to come by: for many reviewers the play was the thing which drew them to Canterbury or the Mercury; there is also the impression that the actor was not so much seen as playing a role as taking part in an act of celebration. But Conrad Aiken found him 'superb' and Charles Morgan in *The Times* for 17 June 1935 after praising the vigour and variety of the choral speech, went on:

Becket himself has a corresponding freedom from stately
monotony. As represented by Mr Speaight he is extraordinarily
rich in spiritual vitality, and one has an impression . . . of being
admitted to his mind and seeing the world with his eyes.

Dermot Morrah, reviewing the Mercury presentation in *The
Times* of 2 November, also linked Speaight with the Chorus's
efforts:

One of them in particular can speak verse as purely as Mr
Robert Speaight himself; and Mr Speaight shows once more that
he has no superior in that art on the London stage. Mr Eliot has
given him an opportunity that any actor might envy, to portray
mind and spirit together at war with the innermost temptations
that can beset the heroic soul; and he plays the part with a fire
repressed until it is transmuted into light.

A Becket who cannot give Eliot's lines their full value is
unlikely to succeed, and Robert Donat who played the
Archbishop at the Old Vic in March 1953 also had a high
reputation as a speaker and reader of verse. Unfortunately,
he was subject to prolonged bouts of asthma which led to an
early retirement from the stage and death at the age of 53;
before *Murder in the Cathedral* he had been absent from the
stage for 6 years. E. Martin Browne found him 'a gentle
Becket', but perhaps Donat was over-deliberate in speech
and tended to iron out the internal conflicts and struggles
that the saint underwent on the route to

Now is my way clear, now is the meaning plain:
[p. 258]

perhaps a matter of temperament, perhaps a need to conserve
his energies, perhaps some uncertainty as to the precise stage
at which Becket regained his convictions, was responsible for
the 'smoothness' of Donat's playing, but about his stature
and presence there could be no reservations. Taller than
Speaight and far more physically impressive, Donat gave a
severe and grave performance which gained in strength partly
because of the bodily ordeals he had undergone and was to

undergo in the next five years. *The Times* for 1 April 1953 was justly complimentary:

> Mr Robert Donat presents a Becket whose warm humanity shines attractively through his ecclesiastical dignity and whose beauty of diction gives us no cause to dwell on a certain lack of vocal power to be remarked at moments of crisis. His commanding presence always seems to become his setting . . .

Donat was an elderly-sounding 48 when he played Becket, Richard Pasco a more dynamic 46, and it is perhaps important to have an actor for the part who does not appear too smoothly archiepiscopal and unravaged. Pasco's flattish face with its ringed, somewhat staring eyes suggested a haunted man, and one whose early life had indeed been devoted to 'mirth and sportfulness' although the convincingly lousy hairshirt may also have played its part. Compared with Donat's, this was certainly a Becket who knew the world and the world's vices, and this lent authority to the Tempters and made the battle to resist their blandishments more credible. As David Jones remarked after speaking to those who had seen Donat, Pasco 'managed to express far more tension and uncertainty before choosing the road to martyrdom'. One felt that the player had gone as far as it was possible to go with the *acting* of Becket and making him a person by putting the 'flesh' which Speaight desiderated on to the skeleton which Eliot had fashioned. But vocally, too, Pasco could stand comparison with his predecessors; to quote Martin Esslin in *Plays and Players* for October 1972: 'Richard Pasco surpasses himself in the part of Thomas Becket: his voice is beautiful in itself and he modulates it superbly.'

Less enthusiasm was voiced, however, about the handling of the Chorus, and the debate on this queston is central to the understanding of the chief problem in staging all Eliot's plays, namely the balance to be struck between realism and ritual stylisation. Part of the difficulty is that Eliot has defined his chorus socially by having them allude to themselves as 'the scrubbers and sweepers of Canterbury' and so depriving them of that impersonality which is a

feature of their use in Greek tragedy. From the first this
seems to have created a dichotomy, as Speaight remembered:

> They spoke beautifully, but they remained middle-class young
> women from South Kensington. Nothing more remote from the
> medieval poor could have been imagined ... They gave one
> Eliot's poetry without ever being able to give one Eliot's people.
>
> ('With Becket ...', p. 186)

Eliot clearly envisaged a 'folksy' Chorus – Speaight recalls
that he liked a set of Irish voices heard in Dublin – but in
some ways this is spurious too; the language and the
sentiments of the Chorus are scarcely those of 'scrubbers and
sweepers'. Yet, as Martin Esslin argued over the 1972
interpretation:

> the seven ladies of Canterbury sound as though they were
> reciting poems of T. S. Eliot which they had just learnt by heart.
> Their voices are far too middle class, their intonations far too
> Third Programme [the BBC's 'cultural' radio channel] to make
> them believable medieval paupers of Canterbury. Why, then, try
> to make them dress up and behave as though they were just
> that?   (*Plays and Players*, October 1972)

The problem for Esslin was compounded by having the
Chorus's lines distributed among the several members of the
ensemble, having the effect necessarily of 'characterizing' the
individual figures and making realistic dialogue of the text.
But this was a tradition with the play which went back to
Miss Fogarty and the original production; as she wrote:

> The great peculiarity of Eliot's choric work was the way
> individual threads of character ran through the whole of his
> choruses. ... The problem was to find the exact number of
> speakers needed for each phrase in the chorus, and very soon we
> realised that we were doing not strictly choral work – but
> orchestral work; each speaker had to be like an instrument, in
> harmony with the other voices during the ensemble passages, but
> repeating a recurring phrase in an individual tone ....
>
> (Quoted in Marion Cole, *Fogie*, 1967, p. 165)

But the difficulty is that even when lines are allocated to soloists or duettists, they still remain far from being the plausible utterances of medieval peasants: Esslin argued for an abandonment of all pretensions to realism, and blamed Hands for sticking to 'the traditional compromise of figures who try to pretend they are real characters while at times unaccountably breaking out into unison'; this critic approved of the decision to give the Chorus leader alone the speech beginning 'I have smelt them, the death-bringers', 'writhing in a mixture of orgasmic lust and birth pangs'; for Esslin here the verse became 'intelligible and dramatic' though even then, while excessive volume was avoided,

> the attempt to *paint* every image vocally was overdone and therefore devoid of the realities of disgust and horror – too beautifully, too artily spoken, in fact, too much the conventional poetry-voice. (op cit)

Certainly this charge could also be levelled against the rather stately 1953 Old Vic Chorus, but there (if the evidence of the gramophone record reflects theatrical practice), the majority of the lines were spoken solo, with a minimum of unison work.

The Helpmann production raises the issue of mobility; should the Chorus be unrealistically static but an unobtrusive presence, or should they add to the variety of the stage picture by 'acting' in various ways, including employing gesture and movement? The Greek chorus danced, and Helpmann as a dancer and choreographer was naturally able to devise and direct routines for his Women which won *The Times* critic's approval:

> He regulates the stage movement with the utmost nicety of judgement, he handles the chorus with a quick balletic inventiveness which doubles its value . . . (1 April 1953)

Some felt this to distract unduly from the words, however, and in the RSC production, a similar attempt to impose momentum merely added to the sense that the Chorus was

neither an abstract unified force nor a group of genuine
medieval beggarwomen; the editor of *Plays and Players* for
October 1972 observed:

> When Hands uses the play as a ritualistic pageant, the effect is
> electrifying; however, neither he nor the actors know what to do
> with the chorus and they quickly degenerate into a gaggle of
> droning hags

and his reviewer glossed the point:

> The need to treat the chorus realistically . . . produces a plethora
> of movement, an unnecessary restlessness in the staging: a wholly
> stylised chorus could be very still, like a frieze on the borders of a
> painting; being real people, these women have to move about a
> great deal. But as the text does not adhere to any realistic
> time sequence, this merely results in useless marching and
> countermarching.

The problems of reconciling two different dramatic styles
are also acute in *The Family Reunion* and *The Cocktail Party*,
although they reveal themselves in different ways to their
manifestation in *Murder in the Cathedral*. We have already
touched on the pressures exerted in *The Family Reunion* on
those playing the relations who have to switch from character-
parts to choric utterances, and seen how Eliot placed fewer
obstacles in the way of the players of 'the Guardians' in *The
Cocktail Party*. However, Reilly in particular has to operate on
two plains, and it is in the part of the psychiatrist that much
of the histrionic interest of the piece lies.

Alec Guinness won high praise when he created the role in
1949, Hugh Kenner asserting when reviewing *The Elder
Statesman* for *Poetry* in October 1959 that only he

> who brings to a part his own ritual of furtive detachment, seems
> ever to have been conspicuously intimate with an Eliot character,
> less by empathy than connaturality.

Certainly the critics were aware of the high quality of
Guinness's performance, even if at 37 he was a little young

for the part. When he revived the role nineteen years later, Frank Cox in *Plays and Players* for August 1968 felt his 'definitive Uninvited Guest' had gained in maturity on what was originally 'an unmatchable interpretation'. He went on:

> Bearded now, and solider in build than before, Guinness negotiates the verse with complete mastery, and there can be nowhere a more suitably tactful and authoritative exponent of that testing second act than he. . . .

Earlier Robert Speaight himself had seen Guinness's Reilly in religious terms when he wrote in the *Tablet* for 3 September 1949 that 'Sir Henry might so easily have become an ethical bore, sugaring his pills with whimsy. But with Mr Guinness we are worlds away from ethics; this is the confessional, and the choice is between the loss of personality and the love of God.' On the same date in the *New Statesman* Desmond Shawe-Taylor said:

> Mr Guinness lends an extraordinary sort of comic authority to Sir Henry: with his long quizzical face, his long straight nose, his great searching eyes, his sardonic humour and his impressive delivery, he conveys (am I wrong who never saw the Great Man?) something of the magnetism of another Sir Henry [i.e. Irving, the famous Victorian actor].

Unfair comparisons were bound to be drawn between Guinness and Rex Harrison who succeeded him in the part for the London run, but the former light-comedy actor was in fact a skilled enough player to reshape the mould in which the role was conceived. Harrison may have played a little too much for laughs – Eliot mildly remonstrated with Browne on the way Reilly sneaked an extra gin when Edward was letting Julia in – but *The Times* felt that he gave Reilly a less cryptic and more professional air than Guinness chose to, which made 'the Guardians' more easily accepted. T. C. Worsley in the *New Statesman* for 13 May 1950 also felt that the advantages were not all with Guinness:

> That Mr Harrison is miscast goes without saying. . . . It is

impossible to compare him with Mr Guinness; they are opposites.
Mr Guinness was rigid, decisive, imperial; Mr Harrison is soft,
tentative, engaging; Mr Guinness commanded his way through;
Mr Harrison charms his way along. But in the consulting room
scene in the second act he does impose a kind of ascendancy.

Harold Hobson, too, for the *Sunday Times* felt that the actor
gave 'a fine, grave, sincere performance, lightened only by a
slight smile' and only needed a touch more assurance to be
the 'man-of-the-world' Reilly, though never the 'man-of-
another-world'. Again, the problem of spanning the 'two
worlds' of all Eliot's plays is presented.

Hobson's review mainly dwelt on the unexpected pleasure
of seeing how good Margaret Leighton was as Celia, given
what were then felt to be her 'agreeable tinsel charms' which
the early part of the play displayed admirably enough.

It is later, when this bruised butterfly beats with an eagle's
wing over

the rarified heights of the great mountains of human aspiration,
that one expected Miss Leighton to fail ... when Mr Eliot
comes to talk of saintliness, as he does in Celia's consultation
with Sir Harcourt Riley [sic], the phrase, the incident that would
bring the consciousness of sanctity into our minds with the flash
of illumination escapes him. He talks about, he ranges round,
but he does not create, saintliness.

   Miss Leighton does: or very nearly. I don't know how. It may
be the expression, the wan, searching, dedicated look upon her
face; it may only be the complete avoidance of self-righteousness
that distinguishes her performance from that given elsewhere, in
the same part. . . .

(Quoted in Harold Hobson, *Verdict at Midnight*, 1952, pp. 183–4)

The last reference, however veiled, must be to Irene Worth,
the American actress who had created Celia some nine
months earlier at Edinburgh. Leighton at 28 was perhaps a
more suitable age for Celia than Worth at 36, but this was
not the essence of the difference. There was a robustness and
commonsense quality about Irene Worth, a capability which
was to make her Helena in *All's Well* for Tyrone Guthrie in

Ontario (with Guinness as the King) memorable, but she
failed to suggest the vulnerability beneath the social poise
which Leighton found. Nevertheless, in a cast which many felt
erred on the side of gentility, her warmth and directness were
not entirely out-of-place.

When Eileen Atkins came to portray Celia at Chichester
in 1968, her ability to match Irene Worth's capacity to
suggest sincerity and depth of feeling was commented on
favourably, but Frank Cox in *Plays and Players* for August
1968 felt that she was better suited by age and appearance to
the role (Atkins was in fact 34!). 'Dressed in white and
highlighted by a white spot [another detail which suggests
the relinquishing of strict naturalism] . . . with enormous
conviction in those saucer-eyes', this Celia was marked by
'a seriousness which never spills over into drabness'; Atkins
was 'every inch Eliot's "saint"' without making spectators
feel that she was less than a human being for all her exalted
calling.

The problem, however, remains in playing any of the roles
in Eliot's plays with a naturalistic setting; exaggerate the
spiritual significance of what you represent and you will fail
to convince audiences that you are a member of the same
species as they; accentuate the common humanity which
binds you to your fellows, and you run the risk of puzzling or
antagonising them when you speak or act outside the norms
of everyday conduct. In his *Drama from Ibsen to Eliot* (1952)
Raymond Williams complained that too many of the cast in
the 1950 production of *The Cocktail Party* put too much
'characterization' into their roles, thus losing the 'poetry' of
their deeper significance. This may be an ultra-purist
viewpoint, but it has analogies in the question of how to
treat the Chorus in *Murder in the Cathedral*. Actors in Eliot
who are over-aware of the serious connotations of their roles
can fail to make them 'work'; for example, Robert Flemyng's
Edward in 1949 was almost too cold a fish and too dull to
allow Edward's humanity a chance to emerge so that he
could seem a man worth redeeming; Michael Aldridge at
Chichester in 1968 gave him a more engaging air, making
him both more pathetic and more humorous, so that while

he remained discomfited for much of the time, he never seemed aloof or unacceptably austere. The danger with this approach, however, is that *The Cocktail Party* can then come to seem little more than a publicity tract for the Marriage Guidance Council.

11 THE CRITICS' VERDICTS

As several of the books published in the present series demonstrate, it is impossible to assess literary and theatrical factors in separate portions of the brain: problems of text often create problems of performance, especially with an author like Eliot, whose dramatic productions create fascinating but often insoluble puzzles for actors and directors. There was often, as we have seen, more interest in what Eliot had just written than in the theatrical means being employed to aid its realisation, and the sharp dichotomy between lovers of poetry and lovers of drama was often manifested in the debate between those who felt that the Thespians had ruined a great masterpiece by trying to stage it, and those who argued that Eliot never truly understood the needs of the theatre. It is hoped that neither of these views will be heard again, at least not in their cruder forms, although it must be admitted that there is perhaps a grain of justification for both of them.

Let us begin this brief attempt to summarise some of the issues which Eliot's plays involve us in by stating that his *are* plays for performance, however little some commentators feel they lose if translated into radio dramas. He intended them to be set forth by live actors for public viewing, and took endless pains to fashion them to those ends: he was not a playwright like Byron who despised the staple requirements of the living stage and wrote his pieces in defiance of popular taste. Indeed, as we know, Eliot perhaps *over*-exerted himself to disguise his comedies of spiritual enlightenment as familiar examples of well-loved genres, and so alienated saints and sinners alike. But he did not hold himself aloof from the theatrical preferences of the public.

On the other hand, it is legitimate to say that he did not possess the characteristics of a natural dramatist; it has frequently been said that he heard his plays in his head, rather than seeing them in his mind's eye. He was after all a poet before he was a playwright; he could perhaps handle the speaking voice as the soliloquies which are *The Love Song of J. Alfred Prufrock* or *The Journey of the Magi* ably show. But while this permitted him to give an assured and authoritative note to Becket's solos or the choruses in *Murder*, it took Eliot longer to learn how to handle dialogue and to build a scene by this means and this alone. And even when he did so – and the exchanges between Harry and Mary in *The Family Reunion* and that between Edward and Celia in Act One of *The Cocktail Party* show the degree of competence he achieved at it – he needed to be persuaded by Browne over the latter scene that uninterrupted duologue can impose a strain on spectators. The wisdom of allowing 'natural breaks' to occur by bringing Julia and Alex in at intervals not only provides variety, but also builds up the tension between the lovers. In Act Two no such diversions proved possible, and some people complained that the lengthy interview between Reilly and Edward, succeeded more or less immediately by that between Celia and Reilly, was too much to take. Perhaps the latter dialogue is sufficiently intense to justify its static nature – Browne felt that Guinness and Worth established such an excellent *rapport* that the entire thirteen minutes' worth of text could be played with both actors seated throughout – but the rarified conceptions, both emotional and spiritual, that are under discussion meant that for many the time dragged, despite Guinness's riveting intensity and power. On the other hand, it is hard to visualise how a session in a psychiatrist's consulting room could be made fluid or fast-moving, without introducing some false note of histrionics or sensationalism.

And this of course brings us back to the central point, the relationship between the need to root the stuff of Eliot's

drama in some form of everyday reality, be it medieval or
modern, and the importance of keeping audiences informed
that the primary focus of attention will not remain for ever
on the mundane level. In the world of *Murder in the Cathedral*
there is rather less of a problem – and if the line about
'scrubbers and sweepers' can be cut it is reduced ever
further – in that the world of the Middle Ages cannot ever be
a particularly 'real' one to the denizens of the twentieth
century, so that its basis in experience is already impaired,
and we approach the gulf between 'now' and 'the hereafter'
without too many presuppositions about the 'now'. One
suspects that perhaps the best mode of presenting *Murder in
the Cathedral* would be to aim at a kind of timelessness
whereby the medieval elements would not be insisted upon
too strongly, though the religious dimension – saints, martyrs,
introits, the Pope – is not easily flushed away. But Hands's
production demonstrated that one cannot insist too
realistically on too overt a periodicisation.

But with the later plays it is different. Eliot himself was
quite insistent on the degree to which they were to be
identified with the 'usual product'. On 6 May 1949 and
again on 2 July he instructed Browne:

> The supernatural element, if we call it that, ought to be not at all
> evident: this play, it seems to me, needs a much more matter-of-
> fact and realistic setting [than *The Family Reunion*], and the
> costumes should not be too stylised and harmonious. . . . An
> *imposed* symbolism in the decor would be painful. What I want is
> something superficially at least purely realistic – the rooms what
> they would be in a perfectly naturalistic play. If the decor
> conveys any more than that, it should only come from the genius
> of the designer . . .   (*The Making of T. S. Eliot's Plays*, p. 232)

Yet the fact remains that to proceed in this manner can run
the risk that the piece may 'split down the middle' at those
points when the play's central concerns pass from the
temporal to the eternal, or from the material to the spiritual.
Audiences are notoriously prone to preferring to know where
they are, and excessive naturalistic detail may be as unhelpful
to their response to the 'extra-terrestrial' dimension of *The*

Cocktail Party as a forbidding or pretentious attempt to stress that the Chamberlaynes and Celia do not exist simply on the level of Knightsbridge flats and Harley Street specialists.

This curiously enough also relates to the question of dramatic language; in *Murder in the Cathedral* Eliot was writing a special type of drama in a special idiom, as he freely admitted himself. There was no attempt necessary or striven after to create a language which people would accept as that of everyday; the play was located in the Middle Ages; it was an act of celebration for a saint of the Christian Church; it set out to recreate in terms of Christian liturgical conventions the auspices of ancient Greek tragedy. So it might reasonably blend the cadences of a variety of English literary works with the rhythms and images of biblical literature to produce a medium novel and yet not unfamiliar to more than a minority of those who witnessed the earliest performances.

But Eliot was honest enough and experimental enough to realise that he could not continue to find subjects suitable for treatment in his newly-invented style; he must next essay the much harder task of creating a more flexible mode capable of spanning a range of demands which extended from ordinary unassertive commonplaces to matters of weighty, emotional, passionate, intuitive or metaphysical discourse. But for several critics the unfortunate irony was that by insisting on this dry, unemphatic, 'transparent' medium Eliot was needlessly hampering himself; Brooks Atkinson wrote of *The Cocktail Party* in the *New York Times* for 29 January 1950:

> . . . to me, it is insufficiently poetic. It needs more eloquence, passion and imaginative courage. Mr Eliot is writing about things that cannot be adequately expressed in the earth-bound, cerebral style he has deliberately chosen for his experiment . . .

The 'daunting reticence' already complained of by J. C. Trewin, the lack of 'excitement, ring, theatrical attack', was deplored by others who felt that a great wordsmith had traded his anvil for the key of a morse-code transmitter.

While Eliot disappointed those who felt his later dramatic verse was an attenuated and colourless invention, others took

him to task for writing in verse at all, pointing out that the
most stimulating passages in *Murder in the Cathedral* had in
fact been the prose sermon and the Knights' addresses.
Kenneth Tynan, writing in 1954 and anxious to scotch the
notion that 'there are certain subtle and rarefied states of
being which can achieve theatrical expression only in verse',
made a telling point:

> Nobody wants to banish luxury of language from the theatre;
> what needs banishing is the notion that it is incompatible with
> prose, the most flexible weapon the stage has ever had, and still
> shining new. . . . One of the handicaps of poetry is that penumbra
> of holiness, the legacy of the nineteenth century, which still
> surrounds it, coaxing us into tolerating sentimental excesses we
> would never forgive in prose:
>> O God, O God, if I could return to yesterday, before I thought
>> that I had made a decision. What devil left the door on the
>> latch for these doubts to enter? And then you came back, you,
>> the angel of destruction – just as I felt sure. In a moment, at
>> your touch, there is nothing but ruin.
> Exit, you might expect, into snowstorm; but you would be
> wrong. The lines come not from Victorian melodrama but from
> *The Cocktail Party*, printed as prose.
> (*Curtains*, 1961, Penguin edn [as *Tynan on Theatre*], 1964, pp. 332,
> 333–4)

It could be argued further that the linguistic clichés of a
debased theatrical form were not the only stain on Eliot's
dramatic originality: *Murder in the Cathedral* is *sui generis*, but
The Cocktail Party is not only indebted to the drawing-room
comedy syndrome for its superficial aspects alone. In Reilly's
'mending' of the marriage between Lavinia and Edward
there is more than a touch of the worldly-wise *raisonneur*
beloved of late-Victorian and Edwardian dramatists like
Pinero and Henry Arthur Jones, who reconciled estranged
couples and preached the doctrine of 'give and take' which
(in exalted form admittedly) is all Sir Henry offers. It is also
true that when Eliot conveys on a cerebral and mildly
mystical plane, a dramatist like Terence Rattigan was
promulgating on a less lofty (and some might say less

pretentious) one; 'the best of a bad job' is what so many of
Rattigan's characters were urged to accept in a range of
plays of roughly the same vintage – *The Browning Version, The
Deep Blue Sea* and *Separate Tables* among them – a domestic
philosophy which chimed well with the 'stiff upper-lip'
bourgeois stoicism of the decade which followed the end of
World War II. It is worth bearing this in mind when large
claims are made for the sanity and humanity of Eliot's view
of sound material relationships. Yet, if we find Eliot's
treatment of this ideal coming to mind more persistently
than Rattigan's, it can surely only be on the grounds that
Eliot manages to summarise its essence in speech more
tellingly than his counterpart:

> They do not repine;
> Are contented with the morning that separates
> And with the evening that brings together
> For casual talk before the fire
> Two people who know they do not understand each other . . .
> [p. 417]

And that ability to make memorable phrases may be
fundamental to the continuing life of Eliot's dramas.

But admitting such a thing may be supplying ammunition
to those who still maintain that Eliot's plays are really
chamber-dramas, that they suffer from a lack of theatricality
which is fatal to their success; the 1968 revival of *The Cocktail
Party* and the 1972 *Murder in the Cathedral* went some way
towards dispelling that slur, but perhaps not quite far enough
to put the issue beyond doubt. There is still the charge that
he never really learnt how to construct a completely satisfying
play; that after Part I of *Murder* there is no dramatic tension,
because Becket has resolved his conflicts – and even then it
could be argued that Eliot dodges the really important
dramatic question as to how Becket shifts his position from
one of doubt and disillusion to the confident assertion that he
has conquered his final temptation. In a similar way, a
number of readers and spectators have sensed that the third
act of *The Cocktail Party* is an afterthought – Eliot originally

had it marked as an Epilogue – because once again 'all the great things are over' in that one of the main protagonists has disappeared from mortal view. Yet Celia was never as intimately present in the play as Edward, and her absence is sufficiently striking for us to sense that the gap in the ranks of the original partygoers is significant. It might also be said, too, that Eliot wants 'the great things' to be assimilated into the world of 'telegrams and anger', and to demonstrate that mundane activity cannot cease simply because a saint has been mixing with ordinary mortals for a brief period. The final act allows the purpose of Celia's life on earth to be pointed up, and gives us the satisfaction of seeing that our most plausible proxies in the action – Edward and Lavinia – are also in the position of enjoying a sense of achievement, even though it may be on a humbler level than that of their former friend.

Many of those who read or study or witness these plays will remain unconvinced as to their quality; Eliot identified too strongly with the socially privileged and the spiritually convinced to make a firm appeal across the widest spectrum of tastes and beliefs. For many the worlds he created were chilly, morally bleak or doctrinally forbidding, and his leading characters uninviting. Desmond Shawe-Taylor in the *New Statesman* for 3 September 1949 detected something of the Edward of Act One and Act Two in Eliot himself:

> he seems incapable of love: of warmth towards the particular, as opposed to a diffused benevolence. The muddy adorable substance as it is lived seems curiously far from this fragile community, and I find something faintly repellent in the quiet smiles and antiseptic wisdom of Sir Henry and his two pals.

Some of these strictures were perhaps dispelled in the last play, *The Elder Statesman*, written when Eliot had found personal joy in his late second marriage to Valerie Fletcher. Even then, he cannot completely evade Richard Findlater's charge that his plays are made with ideas rather than with human beings, and that the thesis precedes the characters who are its puppets.

But when one considers the distance Eliot had to travel to

create a viable poetic drama and a new language to express it in; when one notes his persistent desire to make fresh attempts on a task which he was the only writer of his time to essay (namely, to capture the commercial stage for verse and for serious ideas); when one thinks of the vice-like grip in which the English theatre of his day was held by naturalism and light amusement in partnership; when one realises that, had he not achieved a lasting reputation as poet and critic, his work in the theatre might have seemed a major achievement and not a mere complement to his authoritative work, one cannot without seeming unduly grudging refuse to give at least a qualified fanfare of a decorously muted kind to the dramatic work of T. S. Eliot.

READING LIST

For reasons of space, only works central to a discussion of Eliot's *Murder in the Cathedral* and *The Cocktail Party* are included. Place of publication is London, unless otherwise stated. Items represented in Hinchliffe's *Casebook* are asterisked(*).

Peter Ackroyd, *T. S. Eliot* (1984), esp. chs 11 and 14.

Patricia Adair, 'Mr Eliot's "Murder in the Cathedral"', *Cambridge Journal*, 4 (1950), 83–95.

William Arrowsmith, 'English Verse Drama (ii): "The Cocktail Party"', *Hudson Review*, 3 (1950), 411–30.

——, 'Transfiguration in Eliot and Euripides', *Sewanee Review*, 63 (1955), 421–42.

Caroline Behr, *T. S. Eliot: A Chronology of his Life and Works* (1983).

Bernard Bergonzi, *T. S. Eliot* (1972; 2nd edn, 1978) esp. chs IV and VI.*

J. T. Boulton, 'The Use of Original Sources for the Development of a Theme: Eliot in "Murder in the Cathedral"', *English* (Spring 1950), 2–8.

M. C. Bradbrook, *English Dramatic Form* (1965), ch 9 ('Eliot as Dramatist').*

E. Martin Browne, 'The Poet and the Stage', *Penguin New Writing*, 31 (1947), 81–92.

——, 'The Dramatic Verse of T. S. Eliot' in Richard March and Tambimuttu (eds), *T. S. Eliot: A Symposium* (1948), pp. 196–207.

——, 'From *The Rock* to *The Confidential Clerk*', in Neville Braybrooke (ed.) *T. S. Eliot: A Symposium for his Seventieth Birthday* (New York, 1958), pp. 57–69.

——, 'T. S. Eliot in the Theatre: A Director's Memories', in Allen Tate (ed.) *T. S. Eliot: The Man and His Work* (1967; Penguin edn., 1971), pp. 119–35.

——, *The Making of T. S. Eliot's Plays* (Cambridge, 1969).

—— [with Henzie Browne], *Two in One* (Cambridge, 1981), esp. chs 4, 5, 9, 14.

Denis Donoghue, *The Third Voice* (Princeton, New Jersey, 1959).

T. S. Eliot, *The Sacred Wood* (1920).*

——, *Selected Essays* (1932; rev. edn, 1934; rev. edn, 1951).*

——, *On Poetry and Poets* (1957).*

Gareth Lloyd Evans, *The Language of Modern Drama* (1977), esp. ch. 8 ('T. S. Eliot – the Dramatist in Search of a Language').*

Helen Gardner, 'The Comedies of T. S. Eliot', in Allen Tate (ed.) (see Browne above), pp. 161–83.*

Michael Goldman, 'Fear in the Way: The Design of Eliot's Drama', in A. Walton Litz (ed.) *Eliot in his Time* (Princeton, New Jersey, 1973) pp. 155–80.*

Michael Grant (ed.), *T. S. Eliot: The Critical Heritage*, 2 vols (1982).

D. W. Harding, 'Progression of Theme in Eliot's Modern Plays', *Kenyon Review*, 18 (1956), 337–60.

Robert B. Heilman, '*Alcestis* and *The Cocktail Party*', *Comparative Literature*, 5 (1955), 105–16.

Arnold P. Hinchliffe (ed.), *T. S. Eliot: Plays*, Macmillan Casebook (1985).

David E. Jones, *The Plays of T. S. Eliot* (1960).

Andrew Kennedy, *Six dramatists in search of a language* (1975), esp. ch. 2 ('Eliot').*

John Lawlor, 'The Formal Achievement of "The Cocktail Party"', *Virginia Quarterly Review*, 30 (1954), 431–51.

Benedict Nightingale, *An Introduction to Fifty Modern British Plays* (1982), pp. 205–23.

Ronald Peacock, *The Poet in the Theatre* (1946).

John Peter, 'Murder in the Cathedral', *Sewanee Review*, 61 (1953), 362–83.

——, 'Sin and Soda', *Scrutiny*, 17 (1950–1), 61–6.*

Kenneth W. Pickering, *Drama in the Cathedral* (Worthing, 1985), esp. pp. 178–95.

Carol H. Smith, *T. S. Eliot's Dramatic Theory and Practice* (Princeton, New Jersey, 1963).

Grover Smith, Jr, *T. S. Eliot's Poetry and Plays: A Study in Sources and Meaning* (Chicago, 1956; 2nd edn, 1974).

William V. Spanos, *The Christian Tradition in Modern British Verse Drama* (Rutgers, New Jersey, 1967).

Robert Speaight, 'Interpreting Becket and Other Parts', in Neville Braybrooke (ed.) (see Browne above), pp. 70–8.

——, 'With Becket in *Murder in the Cathedral*', in Allen Tate (ed.) (see Browne above), pp. 184–95.

Gerald Weales, *Religion in Modern English Drama* (Philadelphia, 1961).

Raymond Williams, *Drama from Ibsen to Brecht* (1968), esp. Part 3, Section 3.

W. K. Wimsatt, Jr, 'Eliot's Comedy [*The Cocktail Party*]', *Sewanee Review*, 58 (1950), 666–78.

Katharine J. Worth, 'Eliot and the Living Theatre', in Graham Martin (ed.), *Eliot in Perspective: A Symposium* (1970).

——, *Revolutions in Modern English Drama* (1972), esp. ch. IV ('T. S. Eliot').

INDEX OF NAMES